# FRANKIE FISH

## AND THE VIKING FIASCO

# ALSO BY PETER HELLIAR

Frankie Fish and the Sonic Suitcase

Frankie Fish and the Great Wall of Chaos

Best Ever Pranks and More!
(written by Frankie Fish & Drew Bird)

# FRANKIE FISH

## AND THE VIKING FIASCO

PETER HELLIAR

Art by
LESLEY VAMOS

Hardie Grant
EGMONT

*Frankie Fish and the Viking Fiasco*
first published in 2018 by
Hardie Grant Egmont
Ground Floor, Building 1, 658 Church Street
Richmond, Victoria 3121, Australia
www.hardiegrantegmont.com

A catalogue record for this book is available from the National Library of Australia



Illustration by Lesley Vamos
Design by Kristy Lund-White

Printed in Australia by McPherson's Printing Group, Maryborough, Victoria.

1 3 5 7 9 10 8 6 4 2

FOR MUM AND DAD.
THANK YOU FOR ALL OF IT.

# A STORY BEFORE WE BEGIN THE LATEST STORY OF FRANKIE FISH

The story you are about to read is a complete fiasco.

It involves Vikings, bears, zombies, slingshots and, of course, time travel.

It involves two time-travelling boys and an old man (with a hook for a hand) who really should know better.

It also involves death.

You have probably realised by now that the boys are none other than Frankie Fish and his one and only friend, Drew Bird. These two scallywags get themselves into more trouble than they know how to handle – it really is one hell of a story.

But where does the story start? Not at the beginning, as you might expect, but way before that – before any of this time-travelling malarkey even began. Although, to get to the start of this story, we need to do a bit of time travelling of our own.

We must go back to *before* Frankie Fish discovered his grandad had invented a **time-travelling machine** known as the **Sonic Suitcase**. *Before* Frankie and his grandad used the Amazing Freido's electric eels to escape from 1950s Scotland. And *way before* Frankie and Drew bottle-flipped their way out of Imperial China.

We must go all the way back to three months before Drew Bird had even started at St Monica's Primary. It was so long ago that Frankie hadn't even been crowned Frankie Fish yet – he was

**Francis Fish Guts** to one and all, and he didn't have a single friend of his own.

Our story begins almost a year ago, on Halloween, when teacher's pet Lisa Chadwick was holding her fourth annual **Halloween Parade**.

Lisa Chadwick was the class prefect, the captain of the debating team, and the future saviour of the universe (that last bit is a direct quote from the first draft of Lisa Chadwick's autobiography, simply titled *Chadwick*). She was also Francis's arch-enemy, for reasons that will soon become clear.

One of Lisa's many, many favourite pastimes was raising money for obscure causes. Some of her most recent projects had been:

1. Disco for Dogs with Diabetes.
2. Fun Run for Fiona (an orphaned budgie).
3. Movie Marathon for Meerkats Who Run Marathons.

Francis strongly suspected that Lisa was only involved with these causes because they came with loads of free publicity. Lisa was on the front cover of the local newspaper almost every week – and that was just for starters. When she raised money for Fiona the budgie, for example, a national TV news crew had come to school and filmed Lisa jogging around the oval with the bird on her shoulder.

'People don't understand how hard it is for a budgie with no parents,' Lisa had said into the camera, her voice trembling and a tear rolling down her cheek. 'I just want to do all I can to help.'

But Francis had seen how everything changed the moment the camera crew had left. 'Stop clawing me, **worm-breath**!' Lisa had snarled at Fiona, swooshing the poor creature off her shoulder and nearly squashing her as she marched away.

The fourth annual Halloween Parade was

supposedly to raise money for lactose-intolerant cows, although Francis was pretty sure that people who genuinely cared about cows didn't usually have an enormous leather pencil case like Lisa did.

Lisa Chadwick's planning of the Halloween Parade was meticulous, and each year the event got bigger and bigger (or **'scarier and scarier'**, as she liked to promote it). Food vans had begun appearing. Local sponsors had jumped on board, setting up information booths about gym memberships and house-cleaning products. And Evan Fiorelli from grade six had even agreed to DJ under his official DJ name, DJ-4-Eva(n).

Of course, when it came to preparing for her own appearance at her own Halloween Parade, Lisa Chadwick went all out. For some reason, Lisa had a penchant for **zombie MASH-ups**, which led Francis to believe that she was in fact a member of the living dead (she wasn't ... not that we know of, anyway). Year after year Lisa would be a zombified version of a famous figure.

**First annual parade:**

Zombified Marilyn Monroe.

**Second annual parade:**

Zombified Queen of England.

**Third annual parade:**

Zombified Carmen Miranda, complete with a rotting fruit salad on her head.

Lisa Chadwick had won first prize for Best Costume each and every year of Lisa Chadwick's Halloween Parade. This wasn't really surprising. Firstly, even Francis had to admit her costumes were pretty amazing. Secondly, Francis was sure that Lisa's costumes were professionally made, which wasn't technically against the rules but really should have been. And thirdly, Lisa's mum was on the judging committee, and she was nearly as painful as Lisa.

Even Francis's big sister, Saint Lou, couldn't seem to beat Lisa Chadwick, though Lou's costumes were always really good and she made them all herself.

Lou never seemed too bothered, though. 'Winning doesn't matter,' she would say with a saintly smile. 'It's just fun being in the parade.'

But Francis didn't feel like that. Not at all. You see, first prize in the competition was a **one-hundred-dollar voucher** for the Cocoa Pit – Francis's favourite cafe.

Francis wanted one of those vouchers so badly. He could imagine himself slurping thickshakes and gorging on giant chocolate-chip cookies after school every day for free. Sure, he'd be snacking by himself, because he didn't yet have a single friend (remember, this was months before Drew Bird came to St Monica's Primary). But still! Those cookies were really good and it would give him something to do every day after school.

Sadly, Francis knew his chances of winning the voucher were slim. The fact was, Francis had never quite nailed a costume. Actually, he hadn't even come close. His parents were always busy at work, which meant Francis had to create his own costumes with whatever he could find around the house – usually about twenty minutes before the parade started. So this is what he'd dressed as:

**First year:** Ghost (white sheet with holes cut out for eyes). No prize. Not even an honourable mention.

**Second year:** Ghost (again ... white sheet with holes cut out for eyes AND arms, so he could reach out and scare people). No prize. Not even a dishonourable mention.

**Third year:** Ghost (this time he tried to add a comedy mash-up element and wore a wig, making him a ghost with a big, black, curly mullet). No prize. No kind of mention at all. Not unless you count the time his parents mentioned how annoying it was that so many of their bedsheets had holes in them.

For the fourth annual parade, Francis had stuck with the ghost theme (he had never been one to learn from his mistakes) but added a bicycle helmet and rode his BMX. Surely a bike-riding, safety-conscious ghost would win the day?

**SURELY.**

But no.

'Yet *another* ghost for Francis Fish Guts?' Lisa Chadwick sneered. She was dressed as zombie Medusa. Francis was sure one of the lolly snakes attached to her wig hissed at him. 'Not to worry, perhaps I can spare you a marshmallow from my **GIANT hot chocolate** with extra marsh-mallows when I win that Cocoa Pit voucher.'

FOURTH ANNUAL HALLOWEEN PARADE
$100
1ST

'I wouldn't accept a marshmallow from you if it was the last one on earth,' Francis snapped (although actually he would have – only **idiots** would turn down the last marshmallow).

The Halloween Parade went as it always did. Parents lined the perimeter of the sports oval, kids ate toffee apples, and people dared to eat whatever was being served up at the sausage sizzle. Every year, there seemed to be more and more people dressed up as zombies. But guess who won first prize for Best Costume?

No prize if you guessed it was Lisa Chadwick in her zombie Medusa outfit.

Francis fumed as Lisa slithered up to collect her fourth **(fourth!)** hundred-dollar Cocoa Pit voucher from Principal Dawson, who had momentarily taken a break from the grill to announce the winners. And if the sight of that wonderful prize being handed (yet again) to the teacher's pet and his arch-enemy wasn't enough to make Francis's blood boil, then what Lisa Chadwick said next definitely did the trick.

As the crowd's applause came to a halt and one of the Mosley triplets (the one dressed as Frankenstein's zombie monster) made **fart noises** under his armpit, Lisa Chadwick cleared her throat. Delicately swishing her green jelly snake zombie Medusa hairdo, she gushed, 'Oh my God, I can't believe I won Best Costume *again*!'

'Yeah, what a surprise,' muttered Francis under his bedsheet.

'I want to thank EVERYONE for getting dressed up to raise money for lactose-intolerant cows,' Lisa went on. 'Well, except for the lame ghosts,' she added snarkily. 'It's almost like they don't WANT to win anything with their dirty old bedsheets!'

And with that she sent a sparkling smirk in Francis's direction and flounced off the stage with her Cocoa Pit voucher.

The crowd was laughing and cheering like crazy – except for one kid, who was standing under his bedsheet costume with a face as red as a sunburnt tomato.

Red with humiliation.

Red with **fury**.

Seething, Francis decided then and there that somehow, some way, he would **win** Best Costume at Lisa Chadwick's fifth annual Halloween Parade, no matter what.

But to find out what that decision led to, you'll simply have to read on.

# CHAPTER 1

# EXTREME TAKEAWAY

Leading up to this year's Halloween Parade, Lisa Chadwick had changed. Yep, she had gone from mildly annoying to completely insufferable. She seemed to think everyone lived in her world – one named Chadwickville. And guess who the Mayor of Chadwickville was? That's right, none other than Lisa Chadwick.

Lisa simply HAD to be at the centre of everything. Frankie and Drew had taken to eating out each and every lunchtime, just to avoid her commenting on the contents of their sandwiches. Of course, it was strictly forbidden for any student to go out through St Monica's school gates during breaks, but Frankie and Drew had found a loophole. Technically, they didn't go through the gates at all. They simply used the Sonic Suitcase to time-travel to wherever they felt like going that day for lunch. Drew called this **extreme takeaway**.

They had eaten paella at a bullfight in fifteenth-century Spain, gorged on ribs in the American Wild West in the 1860s, and even eaten witchetty grubs with Indigenous Australians forty thousand years ago.

But without a doubt their favourite lunchtime option was **pizza in Italy** while taking in a show at the Colosseum. They loved it more than penguins love parades. Frankie wished they didn't have to wear togas every time they went, but Drew maintained it was important to blend in with the locals. And besides, it was a small price to pay to avoid Lisa Chadwick for nearly an entire lunchtime every day. Frankie usually set the co-ordinates on the suitcase so that they returned to school just before the end-of-lunch bell. And he always made sure they came back somewhere well out of view so they could change out of their togas before anyone saw them.

Frankie did this every time ... **except** for today, Friday, the day before Halloween. Today, the boys had been forced to make a rapid exit from ancient Rome. A **lion** had escaped from the Colosseum's main stage and, in his haste to get them out of harm's way, Frankie had accidentally entered the wrong co-ordinates into the Sonic Suitcase. Instead of landing discreetly behind the toilet block, the boys returned **SMACK BANG** in the middle of the school oval – right near a meeting of the Halloween Parade Planning Committee.

Even worse, they landed with such a bump that the suitcase sprang open. In the past this wouldn't have been much of a problem, but recently Grandad had added a new 'feature' to the suitcase so that whenever it opened, it emitted a burst of **rainbow-coloured** light. This didn't seem to have any useful function, but Frankie knew better than to question his cranky-pants grandad about it.

Luckily, Lisa and her faithful followers were too engrossed in their parade-planning to notice Drew and Frankie's rather surprising multi-coloured arrival – but someone else did. Just as Frankie slammed the suitcase shut and hissed, 'Let's get out of here!' to Drew, one of the Mosley triplets spotted them.

Munching on his jam sandwich, the triplet (no-one could tell which one it was) pointed at Frankie and Drew's bizarre attire and guffawed. 'Look who's getting married!'

His brother (not sure which one) joined the guffaws and then chucked his half-eaten apple at Drew's head. Yep, the days of Drew and the

Mosley triplets being bottle-flipping buddies were well and truly over.

'I wish I had my slingshot,' Drew growled. He'd spent an entire weekend loading paintballs into his slingshot and aiming them at the big oak tree in the Bird backyard, and was now quite the marksman (and the tree, along with the surrounding area, was now more colourful than an explosion in an M&M's factory). He wiped some apple off his forehead, accidentally flicking it onto Frankie's face.

'What's going on over here?' demanded Miss Merryweather, who was on yard duty. She marched up to the students who were snickering at Frankie and Drew. Staring at the white sheets wrapped around their middles, Miss Merryweather frowned. 'Why on earth are you two dressed like that?'

'Um, my school shorts are in the wash?' offered Drew, smearing mushy bits of apple off his cheeks.

'Oh, how surprising,' came the voice of class prefect and future President of the World (according to herself and her mum) Lisa Chadwick. 'Fish Guts is dressed as a ghost yet again. Only this time, he has a friend!'

The crowd laughed.

'Please tell me that isn't your costume for my Halloween Parade, Fish Guts,' added Lisa loudly.

'I'll have you know, Lisa Chadwick, that ghosts are COOL –' Frankie began, his cheeks burning.

'Well, you'll have to do better than that if you want *any* chance of winning the **Best Costume** competition,' Lisa scoffed. 'You do realise it's tomorrow, don't you?'

'This is just one idea. We have others,' Frankie insisted.

'Oh yeah, like what?' chimed in the third Mosley triplet.

'Well –' Frankie faltered.

Drew leapt in like a seal rescuing a drowning

ladybird. 'You'll just have to wait and see,' he said boldly. 'But I guarantee we'll have cool costumes and we'll win that hundred-dollar voucher from the Cocoa Pit!'

'OK, that's enough drama for today,' Miss Merryweather said nervously, fearing things were getting a little too heated. The last thing she needed was an uprising like the Grade Four Camp Rebellion of 2014.

'Everybody make your way to class, *now*,' Miss Merryweather added as she marched off, followed by Lisa, who tossed Drew and Frankie a withering look. The other kids trailed along behind – leaving Frankie and Drew alone in their togas.

Frankie clenched his fists and glared at Lisa. 'She's the **worst**!' he muttered.

He could still remember the feeling he'd had underneath that bedsheet last Halloween. How hot he'd felt. How embarrassed. How determined he'd been to win the next competition.

'Whatever it takes, we have *got* to win that Best Costume prize,' said Drew firmly as they put their uniforms back on. 'Otherwise we'll be the laughing stock of the school.'

Frankie nodded. Yep, it was time for a new challenger to rise, and quite clearly white sheets – be they togas or ghosts – were NOT going to cut it.

No, if Frankie and Drew were going to eat for free at the Cocoa Pit forever (or at least up to one hundred dollars' worth), they had to aim high. And little did Lisa Chadwick know just how high they were capable of aiming.

# CHAPTER 2

# WAY BETTER THAN GHOSTS

After school, Frankie and Drew raced home, changed out of their uniforms and grabbed their pocket money, then met up at the Cocoa Pit. They definitely needed a sugar hit and they also needed to work on their plan for winning the Best Costume competition.

The owner of the Cocoa Pit, Connie Cole, brought the boys over their usual treat of thickshakes and a giant choc-chip cookie to share. She smiled when she saw Frankie's notebook, opened to a page headed *Costume ideas for the Halloween Parade*.

'I hope you come up with something really great,' she said. 'I always used to dress up as a ghost for my school's Halloween Parade ... and I never won anything!'

'We're working on it,' said Frankie, grinning at Connie as she put down their snacks. She always seemed to find the biggest of the giant cookies just for them.

'Well, good luck!' said Connie, returning to the counter.

'Vampires,' Drew said, as cookie crumbs fell from his mouth. 'Everyone loves vampires.'

'If people don't come as zombies they will probably come as vampires,' Frankie replied, slurping on his thickshake. 'We need something more original. How about mummies? We can wrap ourselves up in toilet paper.'

'If people don't come as zombies or vampires, they will *definitely* come as mummies,' Drew retorted, picking cookie-mush out of his molars.

'So, no zombies, vampires or mummies ... and I imagine no werewolves either, yeah?' said Frankie.

'Correct.'

'But what if the werewolf was also an awesome basketballer?' suggested Frankie. 'It's from my dad's favourite movie.'

Drew looked completely baffled. 'Yeah, but your dad only likes weird old movies from the 80s,' he replied. 'They're practically prehistoric. Anyway,' he added, taking a big swig of his thickshake, 'to win this prize, we need to think outside of the scary square.'

Frankie nodded. 'Yeah, you're right. Lisa Chadwick's zombie Medusa costume was awesome last year. She scared me even more than she usually does.'

There were rumours that this year Lisa was dressing up as a zombified version of her personal hero, former British prime minister

Margaret Thatcher (who was nicknamed 'the Iron Lady', although she was no relation to Iron Man). Not only that, this zombified Margaret Thatcher was going to be hula-hooping. This was so typical of Lisa: to pick a nerdy costume that *only* the grown-ups would get, and show off with it too. It was like a mash-up on *top* of a mash-up. Frankie knew he'd have to come up with something truly spectacular to beat that.

Something that was definitely **not a ghost**.

Suddenly, Frankie remembered a doco he'd seen on the History Channel with his dad (well, Frankie had watched it – his dad had fallen asleep in front of it). Frankie could not take his eyes away from the screen, and barely even noticed Ron Fish snoring louder than a freight train roaring through a library. The show had featured the **bloodiest**, **goriest**, most **TERRIFYING** things Frankie had ever seen. Which were ...

'**ViKings!**' Frankie exclaimed.

'What – those dudes with the horned hats?' asked Drew uncertainly.

'Vikings are really scary!' said Frankie. '*Way* scarier than vampires and zombies, way scarier even than ghosts and werewolves. Way scarier, because ...' He drifted off, smiling at the straw bobbing in his thickshake like a tiny pogo stick.

'Because why?' Drew urged.

As the straw slowly sunk out of view, Frankie looked up at Drew. 'Vikings are scarier because they were *real*.'

**GULP.**

The two friends stared at each other for a second, then grinned.

'I like it. Let's do it,' Drew yelled. 'Let's be the best-dressed Vikings ever!' He rubbed his hands together gleefully. 'This is going to be so great. Dad's got some old rugs in the garage we can use as fake bear-skin cloaks, and I've got a couple of cricket bats for clubs –'

Frankie stared at Drew Bird and then shook his head furiously. **'No way! Uh-uh. Never!'**

'Why not? We will totally look like Vikings,' protested Drew.

'A piece of old carpet and a cricket bat will not win us Best Costume,' insisted Frankie, going red in the face.

'OK, OK,' replied Drew, trying to calm down his best mate. 'There's a costume place in town, we'll pool our pocket money, and if Lisa can buy *hers* then –'

'No, no, no, no, no. **NO!'**

Frankie took a big breath. He felt like he was about to explain the importance of eating vegetables to a four-year-old.

'We have a time machine, Drew,' he whispered. 'If we really, REALLY want to win Best Costume, we don't have to settle for old carpet and sports equipment. We can get the real deal ... from the **actual Viking era**.'

Drew leant in. 'Are you *crazy*?' he hissed. 'You're the one who's always going on about the rules of time travel!'

'This is different,' Frankie protested. 'All we have to do is go back to the Viking age, *borrow* some authentic gear, win the competition and then we return it.'

It was Drew's turn to go red in the face. 'But –'

'We'll return the stuff straight away,' Frankie assured him. 'This is the only way to win, Drew. And do I have to remind you that this is Lisa Chadwick we're talking about? I'm not losing to her *again*. It's been four years!'

A little voice in the back of Frankie's head said: *We could win without time travel, if we just put our minds to it.* But then he pictured a zombie Margaret Thatcher hula-hooping her way to Best Costume for the fifth year in a row.

*Unless we do something different,* Frankie thought firmly, *Lisa Chadwick will be the centre of the hula hoop AND the centre of attention. It's the only choice we have!*

'Look, I know how dangerous these Vikings are,' said Frankie as calmly and convincingly as he could. 'They are **BLOODTHIRSTY**. They are **BRUTAL**. But –'

Finally, Drew put his hands up. 'Listen to me, Frankie,' he interrupted. 'You survived your face nearly melting off in 1952 in Scotland. We escaped a Chinese dungeon in 1642. *And* we've returned safely from all our extreme takeaway lunches. So if you really want to do this ...' He paused and took a deep breath. '... Then I think we could manage ten minutes to *borrow* a fur and a club in Viking country – wherever that is.' He waved a lazy hand in the air and shot his best mate his trademark grin.

Frankie grinned back as excitement shot through his body. He knew it was a crazy plan, but the idea of beating Lisa Chadwick once and for all, with an **AWESOME** authentic Viking costume, was too tempting *not* to try.

Frankie laughed out loud and slapped the table. 'Looks like we're going to Norway!'

# CHAPTER 3

# MY WAY OR NORWAY?

Frankie and Drew would have time-travelled to Norway right then and there if they could have (after stashing a few more giant choc-chip cookies in Drew's backpack for the ride), but the Sonic Suitcase needed to be recharged before it could do any more impromptu getaways. And the boys had some preparation to do too.

First, they used the last of Drew's pocket money on some decoy plastic Viking helmets from a nearby Two-Dollar Shop (a bargain at only five dollars each). Drew assured Frankie that the plastic horned helmets would help them blend in with the locals until they could borrow some costumes from an actual Viking settlement. Then the boys headed off towards the Forbidden Shed at the back of Grandad and Nanna Fish's house.

The whole way there, Frankie and Drew tried to work out which would be sweeter: a lifetime's supply of thickshakes and cookies, or seeing Lisa Chadwick's face after she was defeated for the very first time by a couple of awesome-looking Vikings. As long as nothing went wrong in Norway, they had this year's Best Costume competition **TOTALLY NAILED**.

Frankie was pretty sure he wouldn't even need to ask Grandad if they could use the suitcase again – he didn't seem to mind them using it for extreme takeaways. In fact, despite time travelling causing all kinds of mayhem for everybody involved, Frankie's grandad was surprisingly supportive of the boys' escapades. Maybe it was because Grandad needed to keep them on side, just in case he ever needed **rescuing** from a historic prison (again).

Or maybe it was so the boys would keep the Sonic Suitcase a secret, because if anyone told Frankie's parents about it, there'd be hell to pay. Frankie also guessed (correctly) that their jaunts through history appealed to Grandad's sense of adventure. After all, who invents a time-travelling suitcase and then bans time travel? No-one, that's who.

Whatever the reason, Grandad was so supportive that he even allowed the boys inside the **Forbidden Shed**. It wasn't long ago that nobody but Grandad had been allowed inside (hence its name). Now, Frankie and Drew went there every couple of days to recharge the suitcase on the Charging Bench, so it certainly wasn't unusual for them to walk straight in without even stopping by the house to say hello to Nanna Fish first. What *was* incredibly unusual was what they saw in the shed that afternoon.

As soon as he swung open the door of the (formerly) Forbidden Shed, Frankie noticed something strange: the place was *clean*. The dust had been dusted, the shelves tidied, the trophies polished. There was even a vase of flowers near the Charging Bench.

'Hmm, that's weird,' remarked Frankie, pointing at the flowers.

'Maybe your nanna put them in here so it would smell less like your grandad?' Drew offered, sniffing the flowers.

'No. Nanna swore she would never set foot in the Forbidden Shed again after being thrown in jail in Imperial China,' Frankie said, putting the suitcase on the Charging Bench. 'Plus it still **smells like farts** in here.'

'Well, maybe your grandad has a secret girlfriend that he goes travelling with instead,' smirked Drew.

'Don't be **gross**,' said Frankie, rolling his eyes. Grandad loved Nanna Fish better than anyone else in the entire world, so there was no way he'd get a girlfriend. Also, who'd want to date a **grumpy** old man like him?

All the same, Frankie had to admit something odd was going on in the shed. There were bits of new equipment that he couldn't quite place. The usual chaos had been replaced by organised rows. And some of Grandad's recent suitcase modifications – like the rainbow light – had been a little *weird*.

Frankie looked around doubtfully. 'Is it possible that Grandad is turning into a neat-freak in his old age?' he suggested.

'Maybe,' replied Drew. 'You never know. Old age does funny things to people. I once saw a one-hundred-year-old woman skydiving on YouTube.'

Just then, Grandad strolled into the shed, his hook glinting in the late afternoon sun.

'Well, well, well, if it isn't a Bird and a Fish messing about in me shed,' Grandad growled, and for a moment Frankie couldn't tell if he was serious or joking.

The old man was wearing sunglasses that Frankie had never seen before. They were a strange-looking pair, with very dark lenses and octagon-shaped frames. He took them off and tossed them onto the Charging Bench. Beneath them, his eyes had a bit of a **sparKle**. That was new, too.

'Have you lost weight, Mr Fish?' asked Drew. 'Or grown some more hair? You look great.'

Grandad grinned a toothy grin, clearly chuffed. 'Thanks, lad. I've been taking better care of meself lately. I used to be quite a handsome devil in me younger days, ye know. The ladies used to call me –'

'Um, Grandad?' Frankie interrupted. 'We're about to pop over to Norway to borrow some Viking costumes for the Halloween Parade.

Anything new we need to know about the suitcase before we charge it and go?'

'Actually, yes!' said Grandad. 'We have added a few new features recently.'

*'We?'* queried Drew, his eyebrows shooting upwards.

Grandad went pink. 'Well, firstly, as ye will've already noticed,' he said, pretending he hadn't heard Drew, or seen his eyebrows, which was impossible, 'the case now emits a gentle rainbow-coloured glow when ye open it.'

Frankie and Drew exchanged a look. Grandad was getting a bit forgetful in his old age, but even so – Frankie was sure Nanna wasn't helping him work on the suitcase.

Was it possible Grandad *did* have a girlfriend after all? That was not only **gross**, but a bit of a worry. The more people who knew about their time-travelling adventures, the greater the chances of someone spilling the beans to Frankie's parents ...

But Frankie decided not to worry about it right now. They had bigger fish – or rather, Chadwicks – to fry. 'Er, do the lights have a function, Grandad?' he asked.

'Not really,' Grandad said. 'They just look pretty. Nothing *wrong* with that, is there?' he added, a little threateningly.

Frankie and Drew shook their heads quickly.

'There's also the new **Circle of Safety** function,' Grandad went on.

'The what of what-what?' asked Drew, screwing up his nose.

'A Circle of Safety,' repeated Grandad, unlooping what appeared to be an extra, extra, *extra* long belt from a hook on the wall. 'When you're ready to depart, you lay something like this on the ground in a circle. Anything within that circle will be transported when you travel. Saves a lot of faffing about with trying to set the protective force field when you want to leave in a hurry.'

Frankie nodded. This new feature would've come in handy when they'd been escaping from the lion in ancient Rome earlier that day. He thought of the lion's **ferocious** **ROAR** and shivered.

'BUT!' Grandad waggled a finger in the air. 'Ye absolutely MUST make sure the circle is complete! If there's a gap, there's a danger that things outside the circle could get transported through time too.'

'Got it,' said Frankie, giving Grandad the thumbs up. 'Drew, you're in charge of the belt, OK?'

'Roger that,' said Drew, wrapping it around his waist several times.

'Anything else?' Frankie asked. He was positively **itching** to get going now.

Grandad nodded. 'Yes, one more. It's still in the development phase so it's not perfect yet, but it might come in handy.' He fished what looked like a padlock out of his pocket.

'Er, Grandad?' said Frankie, slowly. 'I'm pretty sure padlocks have already been invented. Quite a while ago, in fact.'

'It's not a bloomin' padlock, ye idiot!' spluttered Grandad indignantly. 'It's an instant voice translator. Ye can use it when ye don't understand the local lingo.' He turned a key that was sticking out of the bottom of the padlock (um, instant voice translator) and the object began to hum.

Then, in his thickest, **crankiest** Scottish accent, Grandad said: **'Do ye ken now, ye wee doaty numpty?'**

Instantly, a tinny voice floated out of the translator. *Do you understand now, you little idiot?*

DRESS UPS

'That's **very** cool,' said Drew.

Frankie knew his grandad was a good inventor – he'd come up with the Sonic Suitcase, after all – but this was *really* good, especially given that Grandad's memory was a bit unreliable these days.

'Good one, Grandad,' Frankie said. 'We might get to use this in Norway!' He took the translator padlock and clipped it onto the suitcase's handle.

Grandad's expression suddenly changed. He looked a little nervous. 'Eh, Frankie, me lad ... do ye have time for a little chat before ye go flying off to Viking land? There's something I want to talk to ye about. It's, ah, well ... it's on a *personal* subject.'

'Um, we have to get going, sorry,' Frankie said quickly. He definitely did not want to discuss personal subjects with his grandad. *Especially* if his grandad really *did* have a girlfriend! **GROSS!** 'Maybe when we get back, OK? We're in kind of a rush right now.'

Drew glanced at his best friend, but backed him up. 'That's right, the Halloween Parade's tomorrow night,' he explained. 'Nice flowers, though, Mr Fish – I like what you've done with the place.'

'Oh you know, a feminine touch never hurts,' murmured Grandad, vaguely.

'OK, *ew*,' said Frankie, out loud this time. 'Come on Drew, let's bust a move.'

'Off you pop, boys,' Grandad said. 'Stay out of trouble and we'll have a good chat when ye return.'

'Us? Trouble? **Never**!' scoffed Frankie, and giving Grandad one last suspicious look, he dragged the suitcase off the Charging Bench and fled outside with Drew.

He decided to put Grandad and his possible secret girlfriend out of his mind for now, and focus on the very important mission in front of them. 'OK, Drew,' he said. 'You ready for another adventure?'

'I was born ready,' replied Drew. Then he added, 'Actually, I was born nude and covered in goop, but sure, I feel ready.'

Frankie cracked up. 'Good. **Happy travels**!'

# CHAPTER 4

## THERE'S A BEAR IN THERE

Smoke, mud and wet fur.

Those were the three things Frankie Fish could smell as his nostrils took in the scents of his new surroundings.

Lying flat on his back, he opened his eyes and found himself under a very gnarled old tree, surrounded by white rocks.

Frankie shook his head and looked around. The Sonic Suitcase was at his feet and Drew Bird was not far away, face-planting in the muddiest patch of mud this side of Mud Town.

Frankie got to his feet and picked up his plastic Viking helmet, excitement surging through him. 'C'mon, Drew,' he grinned. 'In and out, no mucking about.'

But just as Frankie crowned his head with the two-dollar-shop helmet, a terrifying sight confronted him.

'Drew ...?' Frankie was standing very still. He was more frozen than the Paddle Pop lion would be if it had been covered in ice and abandoned in a freezer.

'Yes?'

'Are you looking at what I'm looking at?' asked Frankie, very quietly.

'That depends,' replied Drew, equally quietly. 'Are you looking at an enormous bear?'

'An enormous bear that's licking its lips and looking straight at us?'

'Yep, that's the one.'

The bear stared at the two boys and gave a low, rumbling **GROWL**. It seemed to be considering its options: *eat now or eat later?*

Drew took a slow, careful step closer to Frankie. 'Do you know if bears are vegetarian?' he gulped.

'Get your slingshot ready, Drew, just in case they're not,' Frankie suggested in a voice so low the words barely escaped his throat.

Drew slowly sneaked a hand into his backpack and rummaged around for his slingshot and a handful of paintballs.

The enormous brown bear watched the boys **shaking** in their non-Viking-approved sneakers. They looked like they might taste a bit funny, but then again, the bear *did* feel like a snack. It took a step closer, and its growl got a little deeper.

'This isn't good,' whispered Frankie. 'Not good at all. Can we PLEASE stop coming face-to-face with dangerous animals?'

'Oh come on, we haven't even come across a **T-Rex** yet,' Drew joked nervously.

'Well, I'm sure it's only a matter of time,'

muttered Frankie darkly.

Neither boy took their eyes off the bear, who had lifted an enormous paw in their direction and was now sniffing the air suspiciously. Frankie thought he saw the fur on its back bristling.

'Hand me that belt Grandad gave us,' Frankie whispered to Drew. 'Time to try out the Circle of Safety.'

Drew gulped and slowly unwound the long length of leather from around his waist.

Keeping his eyes on the bear the whole time, Frankie carefully made a circle around himself and Drew with the belt, ensuring the buckle closed the circle completely.

The bear was growling louder now, and took another step closer.

Sweating, Drew loaded his slingshot and pulled the elastic back. 'I've always liked bears,' he said, his voice shaking like a leaf on a trampoline. 'They're in my top three animals, just behind rhinos and mermaids. I once won a drawing contest in grade two for drawing of a bear riding a rocketship ...'

'Why are you telling me this *now*?' Frankie hissed.

'Because I think it's grossly unfair that I am about to be **eaten alive by a bear**, considering all the hard work I've dedicated to them!'

The bear suddenly tilted its head, and the boys gasped – but it was only looking at the Sonic Suitcase. It had quite clearly never seen anything like it before.

'Come on, bear,' said Frankie through gritted teeth. 'You don't need a suitcase.'

'Yeah, what are you going to pack, bear? You don't even wear clothes,' Drew said in hushed tones.

Frankie knew he needed to set the co-ordinates into the Sonic Suitcase, but it was like his body had turned to marble.

Just then, a branch cracked somewhere

nearby, and the bear turned its head. It must have suddenly remembered that snacking would spoil its dinner, because after a beat it began ambling off in the opposite direction.

'Thank goodness!' whispered Frankie. His heart felt like a shaken-up can of Coke waiting to explode.

Drew lowered his slingshot. 'Let's get out of here, pronto, just in case that bear changes its mind.'

And with that, Frankie unbuckled the clips on the Sonic Suitcase. They were a little stiff and made a loud **snap-SNAP!** noise that echoed through the forest.

Frankie had never noticed how loud the buckles were before, but maybe he had never been in a place that was dead quiet while trying to evade the attention of a big brown bear.

At that moment, the bear halted in its tracks, the fur on its back raising up in alarm. It wheeled around and faced the boys again, this time giving an **angry, full-throated roar**. If there was one thing this bear hated, it was loud, unexpected noises.

'Hurry, hurry!' Drew squealed.

Frankie started typing madly. 'The keyboard buttons are jammed,' he screamed. 'They have mud in them.'

The bear reared onto its hind legs and it was only then that the boys saw the real size of the enormous beast. Looking as tall as a block of fur-covered apartments, it began lumbering back towards them like some hairy, walking nightmare.

As Frankie tried to wipe away the mud from the keys with his T-shirt, Drew loaded a yellow paintball into his slingshot.

'Sorry, Mr or Mrs Bear,' he whispered, aiming at the bear's belly.

**Pop!**

As always, Drew's shot was right on target, stunning the bear with a small explosion of colour. Drew followed up with a red and a blue shot, all hitting the bear in the tummy.

**Pop! Pop!**

Drew didn't feel great about firing paintballs at the bear, but he knew that the paint wouldn't kill it. He just needed to buy them some time.

'How's it going?' Drew panted.

'One of the keys is stuck. We need it to get home –'

The bear was now angry. **VERY ANGRY.** It let out a furious roar that sent chills down Frankie's spine, and began pounding towards the boys as they quivered inside the belt-circle.

'Just get us anywhere away from this very point in time,' yelled Drew.

'OK, this will have to do,' Frankie yelped, mashing the Sonic Suitcase's keyboard and hitting the space bar.

'Happy travels!' Drew called to the furious bear as it leapt towards them – just as he and Frankie disappeared, yet again.

# CHAPTER 5

## THE BOY-MOUNTAIN

The trip was short in almost every conceivable way.

Frankie had been in such a rush to escape the bear's clutches that he wasn't completely sure where he'd told the Sonic Suitcase to take them. A monkey with a blindfold could have hit the keys more accurately in that hurried moment.

This time, the usual stretching and craziness of time travel felt like it lasted a microsecond.

Slightly dazed, Frankie sat up and looked

around. 'This looks like where we were before,' he said.

'It's *exactly* where we were before,' exclaimed Drew. 'There's that weird old tree that looks like your grandad.'

Frankie looked where Drew was pointing. He had to admit that the gnarled old tree *did* look a little like Grandad Fish.

'Um, what's that funny French word Miss Merryweather uses every time we get in trouble?' Drew asked.

*'Déjà vu,'* replied Frankie. 'And yep, it's *déjà vu* all over again.'

Thankfully, this time there was no bear in sight.

'I aimed to arrive about a couple of hours later,' said Frankie. 'I figured the bear would have moved on by then.'

'Well played, Frankie,' said Drew, applauding. 'Hang on, where's the belt?'

Frankie looked around, but the belt had long

gone. 'Oops. I think the bear stole it.'

Drew groaned. 'Stupid bear doesn't even wear pants.'

'Yeah, stupid bear!' Frankie said. 'Oh well, hopefully we won't need it. Let's find some Viking gear and get out of here, fast.'

Despite narrowly surviving a bear attack, Frankie hadn't lost sight of the real prize here: winning Best Costume at Lisa Chadwick's fifth annual Halloween Parade. So, after carefully cleaning the mud off the Sonic Suitcase's keyboard in case they needed to make another **hasty escape**, the boys headed deeper into the forest, their hearts set on finding authentic Viking clobber.

As they walked with their hard plastic horned helmets jolting around on their heads, something struck Drew. 'It's so quiet. A mouse could fart back home and I reckon I would hear it,' he giggled.

Perhaps it was the adrenalin still rushing

through their bodies, but Frankie couldn't help but giggle too. Laughter is contagious, just like the flu. The more one boy giggled, the more the other giggled. Louder and louder it got, until Frankie and Drew were literally rolling on the ground laughing.

Their laughter came to an abrupt halt, however, when a voice reverberated through the trees. It was a voice that spoke in a language completely unfamiliar to the boys' young ears.

'Did you hear that?' Frankie asked Drew.

'Of course I did. I'm right here.' The boys got up from their ROFL positions and looked around like meerkats searching for a taxi.

'Hello!' Frankie half-yelled, half-whispered. 'Is anyone out there?'

There was no reply.

The clouds darkened overhead. In the distance, lightning lit up the sky and thunder crashed.

Frankie and Drew picked up the pace

and pressed onwards, the thunder crashing even louder than before and the lightning illuminating the sky in dazzling bursts. Then, as they rounded a bend in the path that led to a clearing, they came face-to-face with the owner of the voice they'd heard before.

Or face-to-knee, to be more accurate.

This person was enormous – like a man with another man sitting on his shoulders. He was a mountain of a man, with a ginger beard as thick as the Amazon rainforest. He had what appeared to be a bear's pelt wrapped around his shoulders; the rest of his outfit was a curious mix of chain and linen.

'That guy is huge,' Frankie whispered to Drew through chattering teeth.

'Yeah – you would need a chairlift just to reach his chin,' Drew whispered back. And then he did a double-take. 'Hang on ... he's not even a grown-up. Look at his face! He's got pimples. He's a *teenager*.'

'But he's got a beard!' exclaimed Frankie, a little jealously. Frankie himself was nowhere near being ready to shave, even though he was twelve. He'd once woken up and thought he'd grown a luxuriant moustache overnight, but it turned out the cat had fallen asleep beside him with its tail across his face.

The most ominous thing confronting the two time travellers was that this boy-mountain was carrying an **axe**. An extremely large one with an intricately carved handle and a gleaming double-sided blade. A **sharp blade** that was **dripping** with **deep red liquid**.

And if that wasn't bad enough, a moment later Frankie noticed that the oversized man-boy had the same blood-red substance on his hands – and smeared across his face ...

# CHAPTER 6

## ARE THOSE TINY BRAINS?

The Boy-Mountain looked at Frankie and Drew just as curiously (although with considerably less terror) as they were regarding him.

He took a step towards them. Instinctively, Frankie and Drew took a step back, convinced that this might be one of the final movements of their young lives.

Then the Boy-Mountain made a gesturing motion with his hand. Drew took the unauthorised step of making exactly the same gesture back.

'It's been nice knowing you, Drew Bird,' hissed Frankie, as the Boy-Mountain raised an enormous foot. But he didn't step towards Drew. He stepped back. Frankie and Drew were as confused as a rhino waking up on a tram. 'Maybe my hand movement scared him?' whispered Drew.

The Boy-Mountain didn't look scared, though. Not. One. Little. Bit. He did, however, look **slightly less murderous** than before. It was like he was waiting for Frankie and Drew to make a move.

'He wants us to step towards him,' realised Frankie.

'My mum told me never to step towards a stranger in the woods,' hissed Drew, 'especially if they have an axe with blood dripping from it.'

But the Boy-Mountain repeated his hand gesture until, reluctantly, Frankie and Drew stepped forward. Immediately, the Boy-Mountain thumped his feet on the ground and, without really knowing *why* they were doing it, the boys copied.

And then the most remarkable thing happened. Through that ginger forest of a beard, the corners of the Boy-Mountain's mouth curled upwards into a smile. The boys looked at each other and grinned. Frankie felt like a butterfly that has left the cocoon and looked in a mirror.

'I think he's ... **dancing** with us?' he murmured.

'Yeah,' agreed Drew, snickering. 'And it's the way my aunties dance at weddings.'

The next time the Boy-Mountain made a move, the boys promptly copied him. The Boy-Mountain dropped his axe and **roared with laughter**, almost loudly enough to drown out the thunder claps that were still ringing out around them.

If you'd asked Frankie and Drew a week ago what they thought Vikings liked to do for fun, dancing would have never appeared on the list. Yet here they were, dancing with the very first Viking they had ever met.

Finally the Boy-Mountain clapped his hands together, as if to announce that the dancing was finished. He then spoke rapidly in his own language, patting his chest and pointing at Frankie and Drew.

'Um ... we don't speak Viking,' Frankie gulped. 'Only English.' And then he remembered the **translator padlock** Grandad had given him. This was the perfect moment to try it out! Quickly, he put down the suitcase so he could unfasten the padlock from its handle. Then he turned the key in the padlock's base. Just like it had done back in the (formerly) Forbidden Shed, the padlock began to hum.

The Boy-Mountain again thumped his chest and spoke. The padlock crackled like a radio, and Frankie's heart sank. Maybe it couldn't cope with this ancient language? But then the padlock hummed a little louder and a voice came through the clip at the top. *'I am Birger.'*

'That's your name? Birger?' Frankie asked the Viking excitedly. He saw the Boy-Mountain's eyes bulge as the padlock took his question and translated it into ancient Norse. He looked as amazed as an owl at its own surprise birthday party.

For a moment Frankie was nervous that the Boy-Mountain might run away from the weird device, or even attempt to destroy it. But then he seemed to get over his shock. He grinned broadly, nodded and copied Drew Bird's merry jig from moments earlier.

Frankie patted his own chest, then pointed to his best mate. 'I'm Frankie Fish,' he said, 'and this is Drew Bird.'

Birger listened to the translation, then pointed to the boys. *'Frankiifisk,'* he repeated slowly. *'Dru-børd.'*

Then, quite suddenly, he turned and strode over to what looked like a pile of brambles at the edge of the clearing.

'Uh – what is he doing?' asked Drew.

'I'm not sure,' replied Frankie anxiously. He couldn't help noticing that Birger had picked up his axe again. Maybe he was wiping the blood off it so that it would be nice and clean when he used it on them?

A few minutes later, as the thunder petered out, Birger strode back – his hand full of something dripping red that he held out towards Frankie and Drew.

'Are those **tiny brains**?' squeaked Drew nervously, examining the squishy objects in Birger's hands.

'No,' said Frankie slowly, 'I think they're ... berries?'

When Birger heard the translated word he nodded vigorously and spoke rapidly – too rapidly for the padlock to cope. It only managed a few words here and there.

'Yes ... berries ... used ... axe to cut ... brambles.'

Frankie felt a flood of relief. 'So that's not blood on your axe and your face?' he said.

Birger frowned as the padlock translated, and for a moment Frankie was worried he'd made the Viking angry. But then Birger threw back his head and roared with laughter. 'Not blood! Juice! Here ... try!'

Frankie and Drew helped themselves to the juice-laden berries in Birger's hand. They were delicious, and soon their own hands and faces were just as smeared with red as Birger's were. Birger beamed at them. Frankie and Drew beamed back.

They had been in Viking country for less than an hour and it seemed they had already made a friend.

When they'd eaten all the berries, Birger looked at Frankie's plastic hat like he had only just noticed it. He grinned and removed it from Frankie's head, inspected it carefully and then doubled over, chuckling heartily.

'Your hat ... handles!' Birger laughed, putting it on his own head.

'They're not handles, they're horns!' corrected Drew, indignantly. 'And of course it has them. It's a Viking helmet after all.'

Birger shook his head, still giggling. '*Real* Viking helmet ... no horns.'

Wiping away tears of laughter, Birger reached under a nearby bush and produced a massive metal helmet. 'See?' he said, placing it on Frankie's head.

The helmet was heavy and huge

and it definitely had no horns. Frankie's neck was nearly crushed, but his heart swelled with joy. 'I can't believe I'm wearing an **actual Viking helmet**!' he said excitedly to Drew. 'What do you think?'

Drew looked at it thoughtfully. 'It's way too big,' he pointed out. 'It's all dented. It smells like dung.' Then his face broke into a broad grin. 'And it's PERFECT! Lisa Chadwick has no idea what's coming her way!'

Unfortunately, the happy atmosphere was suddenly shattered by a terrifying growl from deeper in the forest, followed by several shouts of terror.

*'Ahh! Ahhhhhhhhhhh!'*

The three boys froze. *What was that?*

Then Birger's face went white. Without another word, he ran towards the call, the little plastic Viking helmet perched on top of his head.

# CHAPTER 7

# WE NEED TWO HELMETS

Frankie and Drew stood frozen to the spot for several moments, not sure if they should run towards the commotion or away from it. But before they could make up their minds, the noise stopped.

'What was *that?*' asked Drew, nervously.

Frankie shrugged, his heart pounding. 'Should we go and check it out?'

To his relief, Drew shook his head. 'Nah, I think Birger sorted it out already. Better to leave

Viking business to the Vikings, I say. We don't want to mess with the fabric of time, right?'

Frankie agreed wholeheartedly. The screams and roars coming from the forest had been bloodcurdling. He was in no hurry to go and find out what had caused them, although he was disappointed that they hadn't had a chance to say goodbye to Birger.

'Well then, let's head home, hey?' said Frankie, picking up the Sonic Suitcase from the muddy grass and patting the real Viking helmet that was still weighing down his head. 'Mission complete and all that.'

But Drew stopped short. 'The mission is **NOT** complete, Frankie.'

'Why not?'

'It's OK for you,' grumbled Drew. 'You have your Viking helmet. But I don't have anything to wear for the Halloween Parade yet.'

'It doesn't matter which of us wins,' Frankie pointed out. 'We'll just share the prize.'

Drew crossed his arms stubbornly. 'I want to look good in the Parade too! We came here for helmets, and I'm not leaving until I convince a Viking to lend me one.'

Frankie briefly considered offering his helmet to Drew, but Birger had given it to *him*, and it was possibly the coolest thing he'd ever received. Besides, Frankie had heard that re-gifting is rude, so ...

'OK, OK, we'll keep looking,' Frankie sighed. 'But only for a few minutes. And if we get eaten by a bear, it's totally your fault.'

'I'll make torches for us from burning sticks,' announced Drew. 'Bears hate fire. It's like their kryptonite. That's why you never see a bear with candles on its birthday cake.'

'Are you sure?' said Frankie sceptically.

'I'm positive!' insisted Drew. 'Bears hate fire the way school teachers hate fun. They hate it the same way Lisa Chadwick hates anything that doesn't involve Lisa Chadwick.'

And with that, Drew got busy making the torch. His dad, Gary Bird, had taken him camping quite a bit over the years and Drew was keen to put those skills to use. He even knew how to start a fire without a match, although this always took him a very long time to do and involved a lot of sweating and swearing.

Frankie started to think it would be easier to duck back to modern times, grab a battery-operated torch and use that instead, except that doing so would wear out the time path. And Frankie knew from experience that wearing out the time path could have **disastrous** results.

Finally, though, as the sun was starting to set, Drew triumphantly presented Frankie with a small but clearly burning torch. Together, the boys began walking deeper into the forest in search of another helmet, an ancient axe or Thor's hammer.

Sadly, after an hour of looking, all they found were sticks, rocks and deer poo. But then, just as

Drew was becoming disheartened and Frankie impatient, they heard something. Voices. Lots of voices, that were either singing, or ... crying.

The boys' curiosity overcame their fear and they walked quickly towards the sound. The voices became louder, and soon an incredible sight appeared before them. 'Wow!' whispered Drew. 'A real **ViKing village**.'

Frankie looked out at the scene. Several low, sturdy wooden buildings, topped with mossy wooden roofs, were contained within a tall wooden fence. Campfires burnt dangerously close to each of these wooden cabins (Vikings certainly seemed to love their wood). To the left of the village was the ocean and along the shore were huge wooden ships that curled up at either end like upside-down moustaches.

And then the boys saw the source of the wailing, singing noise that had led them here. A slow procession of people was making its way through the centre of the village.

Six of the largest men Frankie had ever seen were up the front, carrying something between them.

'What is that?' Drew leant forward, straining his eyes to see. Then he gasped. 'Is that ... is that a *body*?' he exclaimed in horror.

As soon as Drew said it, Frankie could see he was right. The men walked very slowly, wailing and singing mournfully as they trudged along, carrying their sad burden.

Then Frankie spotted two figures right at the back of the procession. One of them was wearing a ridiculously small plastic helmet with horns. 'Look! There's Birger.'

Drew could see them too. 'The guy beside him *has* to be his brother,' he said, pointing. 'He looks just like Birger, only bigger – if that's even possible.'

For a moment, Frankie was pleased to see their Viking buddy again. So happy, in fact, that at first he didn't notice the thing that Birger and his brother were dragging along behind them.

But once he did see it, his joy shrivelled up like a worm on a hot footpath in the midday sun.

It was the lifeless body of a **giant brown bear**, being dragged along on its belly.

# CHAPTER 8

# A VERY BAD THING

A dead Viking. A huge bear carcass. Frankie had a bad feeling that these things were connected to each other, and that *both* things were connected to him and Drew. He hadn't felt this anxious since the time Miss Merryweather had asked him to solve an algebra equation in front of the whole class, and everyone laughed at the word 'bra'.

'Does that bear look familiar to you?' Frankie muttered to Drew.

Drew shrugged. 'One scary brown bear looks pretty much like any other scary brown bear to me,' he said. It was clear Drew had other things on his mind. 'Let's get closer,' he added.

'Uh, I don't think that's such a good idea,' murmured Frankie.

'Oh, come on,' urged Drew. 'We know Birger is a friendly Viking, so he probably comes from a friendly Viking village.'

Frankie wasn't so sure about this logic, but before he knew it, Drew had run out of the forest and towards the tall front gates of the Viking village. Not wanting to be left behind, Frankie raced after his best friend.

As they entered the village, Birger (who was still at the back of the procession) turned around. His face, which had been so cheerful and cheeky when they'd seen him earlier, was now streaked with tears and – Frankie noticed uncomfortably – paint.

Birger regarded them with astonishment

through his red, watery eyes. '*Frankiifisk? Drubørd?*'

Twisting the key in the padlock translator, Frankie said nervously, 'Birger, are you OK?'

Birger shook his head sadly and pointed towards the front of the procession, where the dead Viking was being held aloft. He uttered a single word.

'*Faðir.*'

Frankie didn't need the padlock to translate that word. He'd already guessed what it meant.

'Your father? He died?' Frankie said softly. He felt a lump in his throat like he had swallowed a billiard ball.

Birger nodded slowly. 'Yes, he was attacked while hunting,' the padlock translated. He pointed down at the bear he and his companion were dragging. 'My father was very strong, but that creature was even more powerful. I was with you when the attack happened. By the time I reached my father, it was too late. Usually bears don't cause us any harm. But this bear was very angry. Its fury gave it the strength of twenty animals.'

Frankie was feeling **more and more uncomfortable**.

Just then, the other, larger Viking boy dragging the bear began speaking sharply to Birger. He was too far from the padlock for his words to be translated, but it was clear from his face that he was angry. Birger spoke back rapidly, then turned towards Frankie and Drew.

'This is my big brother, Brynjar,' Birger said. 'He wanted to know why I was talking to strangers without beards, who **smell so weird**. I explained that you can't help how you smell and I told him you are here to attend our father's funeral. That *is* why you came to our village, isn't it?'

Frankie nodded, trying not to be offended at the 'weird' part. Attending the funeral seemed like the least they could do.

Birger wiped his eyes and even managed a small smile. 'I'm glad,' he said. 'It's an honour to have you here with us.'

Frankie felt very sorry for Birger and his brother for their loss. But beneath this, though he wouldn't have admitted it to anyone, he was also a little **awed**. Here he was, wearing an actual Viking helmet, being escorted through an actual Viking village by some actual Vikings, one of whom he and Drew were basically best friends with. This didn't happen every day.

The Viking villagers eyed the boys curiously as they walked along with Birger.

'Stay close,' Frankie whispered to Drew.

'You bet,' replied Drew.

Darkness had fallen by the time the procession made its way through the village and down to the boat-lined shore. A group of Viking women was busy filling one of the longboats with flowers and sweet-smelling grasses; the dead Viking's body was carefully placed into it. Further along the beach was an enormous bonfire, the biggest Frankie had ever seen, and animals were being roasted on spits over the coals.

It was an amazing scene. And then Frankie noticed something even more incredible. The night sky above them began to pulse with colours, flowing and changing ceaselessly like the world's most **impressive laser light show**. It was the *aurora borealis*, also known as the northern lights!

Frankie had learnt about this phenomenon in the Viking documentary he'd watched. He'd immediately vowed that one day he'd see this amazing spectacle for himself. But unfortunately, now was definitely not the right time to enjoy it.

The wailing grew louder as grief-stricken Vikings drank beer, sang mournful songs and hugged each other, thumping each other's backs so hard Frankie fully expected to hear the sound of breaking bones.

Birger stopped by the boat where his father

lay and began to cry loudly. *'Faðir!'* he sobbed.

Brynjar stood on the other side of the boat. He didn't cry, but his face was clouded with fury. This time when he spoke, he was close enough for the padlock to translate.

'You should have been there to protect our father, Birger,' Brynjar said, his voice bristling with rage.

'I know,' wept Birger, tears pouring down his cheeks. 'But this was no normal bear, Brynjar. Look!'

With a tremendous effort, Birger reached his hands beneath the bear and flipped it over.

Frankie and Drew stared down with horror at the creature, whose belly was stained with red, yellow and blue.

# CHAPTER 9

# OH NO, DREW BIRD!

Frankie Fish's head was spinning faster than the spinniest ride at the Spinfest Carnival in Spinsville.

Drew grabbed his arm. 'That's the bear I hit with my slingshot!' he hissed urgently.

'Tell me something I don't know,' muttered back a rather frazzled Frankie as he turned off the padlock for a moment. The pieces of this awful puzzle were fitting together in his mind.

'We made the bear angry. And that must be why it killed Birger's dad!'

'We don't know that for sure –'

But Frankie knew that Drew didn't really believe this. To say this adventure had gone pear-shaped would be an insult to pears.

Nearby, Birger was weeping even louder than before.

It is fair to say Frankie and Drew had NEVER been in a situation like this before: consoling a Viking friend who had just lost a loved one. A loved one whose death was, quite possibly, Frankie and Drew's fault.

This felt like a very adult problem, and Frankie didn't know what to do. His mind was foggier than a bathroom mirror after someone had taken a long, hot shower.

'We need to fix this,' Drew said, through clenched teeth. *'Now.'*

Frankie wished he could snap his fingers and take back their decision to fire paintballs at the bear. But sadly, Frankie's fingers weren't magical, no matter how many times he tried.

'There isn't anything we *can* do,' said Frankie in a low, firm voice.

'What are you talking about?' said Drew angrily. 'We have to make this right! Let's just go back in time and –'

'Stop the bear, Drew?' Frankie yelled back. 'Even if we could do it without wearing out the time path, how we would stop a *freaking bear?*'

Birger and Brynjar were both staring at the boys in astonishment, unsure what had suddenly made them scream at each other.

'We need to undo what we did,' insisted Drew, lowering his voice slightly.

'Drew,' said Frankie, trying to calm down. 'The more we meddle, the more we put everything and everyone in danger. We can't change history any more than we already have by ... by getting Birger's dad killed. Trying to undo this situation could be catastrophic.'

'But –'

'But nothing,' Frankie said, cutting him off abruptly. 'Some knots just can't be untied.'

'So what do we do now?' demanded Drew. 'Just leave? Go home?'

'That's *exactly* what we do. We go home and we **never meddle in time travel** again. What if that had been my dad, Drew? Or yours? This time we went too far.' Frankie felt sick. '*We broke the rules of time travel.*'

Birger came up behind the boys and patted their shoulders with his huge hands. Frankie knew Birger was trying to be gentle, but he felt a little like a tent-peg being hammered into the ground.

He was murmuring something, so Frankie turned the padlock back on. It hummed and crackled and did the best it could to translate Birger's words. 'Don't fight. Come and eat. Hungry makes angry ... much worse ...'

Despite himself, Frankie's tummy rumbled.

He was indeed starving. Night had fallen and all they'd had to eat since arriving was a handful of berries. And the roasting meat did smell delicious.

Drew's tummy was rumbling too.

'Well, maybe we are a bit hangry,' Frankie muttered. 'I guess we've got time for a quick nibble.'

'Nibble?' Birger repeated, raising his eyebrows in confusion.

'He means yes,' Drew replied, keeping it nice and simple. 'You go ahead, I just need to ... find the loo,' he said, giving Frankie a look. He dashed off before Frankie could say he doubted the Vikings even *had* toilets.

Birger led Frankie over to where some logs had been placed around the bonfire. A number of villagers were already there, gnawing on massive hunks of meat, juice dribbling down their arms.

Birger pulled over a massive log as if it were no heavier than a feather-filled cushion, and plonked himself down on it. Then he smiled at Frankie and patted the empty space beside him. 'I am happy you stay, *Frankiifisk*. It shows great respect ... to our *faðir*.'

Frankie gulped, the guilt welling inside him. They hadn't *meant* to change history, but that didn't matter. They *had*, and they'd made a mess of it.

He couldn't help noticing that Brynjar, who was sitting on another log nearby, seemed madder than a snake trying to learn the cha-cha. Frankie had heard of people looking *daggers* at someone, but right now, Brynjar was looking *axes* at him and Birger.

Frankie looked away, and was glad when Drew returned a few moments later. His backpack made a soft **rattly-clunk** as he put it on the ground beside him. Frankie glanced sideways at the bag. Was it his imagination, or was it bulging more than before? Brynjar, Frankie noticed, was staring at it too.

But then Frankie was distracted when a strong-looking Viking woman started handing out what appeared to be T-Rex thigh bones. His empty stomach gurgled loudly. He was *starving*, and Drew was too. When the massive drumsticks arrived, the boys silently tore into them, surrounded by teary, tipsy Vikings.

Frankie did notice, however, that as the Viking woman gave a thigh bone to Brynjar, she tried to speak to him (probably to give him her condolences, thought Frankie). But he brushed her aside and barely ate any of his meat.

When Frankie and Drew could not fit another thing in, they stood up. Frankie felt awful knowing that they had accidentally caused the death of Birger and Brynjar's father, but they'd simply *had* to warn off the bear. And there was nothing they could do about it now.

'We'd better go,' Frankie said. He was half-expecting Drew to put up a fight, but to his surprise, Drew slung his backpack onto his shoulder and stood up too. 'Yep, you're right,' he said quickly. 'Let's go.'

It seemed that for a boy-mountain, Birger was a real softie. He began to weep when he realised they were leaving, and swept them both up into an **extreme hug** that very nearly squished the boys permanently together, like two sticks of plasticine. There was a clanking sound as Birger released them, and Drew tugged at Frankie's arm. 'Come *on*!' he said.

Suddenly there was a shout. A very angry shout, followed by a stream of furious-sounding words that were too fast for the padlock to translate. Frankie turned to see Brynjar charging towards them, **swinging his axe** above his head. Frankie knew they should get out of the way, but he was too scared to move.

At the last minute, Birger grabbed hold of Brynjar's arms, holding him back. Brynjar looked like he couldn't believe his younger brother would dare to stop him like this, and yelled and struggled frantically.

Frankie felt faint with terror. What was going on? Why had Brynjar suddenly exploded like that? As Birger did his best to keep Brynjar away, Frankie realised Brynjar was gesticulating angrily at Drew. Or, more specifically, at Drew's backpack. With a gnawing feeling in his gut, Frankie looked at it. The zip was partially open and through the gap the gleam of something curved and metallic could clearly be seen.

'Oh Drew,' groaned Frankie. **'What have you done?'**

But before Drew could answer, the zip opened up completely and a heavy object fell out. Frankie's heart leapt into his mouth when he saw what it was: a Viking helmet. It was a lot like the one Birger had given Frankie, except that this one was more battered-looking.

Brynjar went completely wild then, and it clearly took every ounce of Birger's strength to keep him away.

Purple in the face, Brynjar pointed to the helmet and then at his own head, screaming with fury. And then it dawned on Frankie exactly what was going on.

'Drew! You *stole* Brynjar's helmet?!'

'I'm only borrowing it!' corrected Drew huffily. 'Which was your idea, remember?

We're going to give them back, once we've worn them in the Best Costume competition!'

'I know,' Frankie yelled, 'but I thought you were going to ask first!'

'We're in the middle of a *funeral*,' Drew shrieked back. 'It didn't seem like the right time to bring it up!'

Finally, Brynjar pushed his full weight against Birger, and Birger toppled over. Frankie's pulse went into overdrive. Now there was nothing between the boys and Brynjar!

'Stay back!' Frankie called out. His voice sounded so thin and shaky compared to Brynjar's impressively deep, powerful tones. Frankie was sweating so hard he nearly lost his grip on the Sonic Suitcase.

'Back me up here, Drew,' he muttered to his mate.

Drew swallowed and cleared his throat. 'I'm sorry, OK!' he said, his voice quivering. 'I swear I was going to bring it back.'

Shaking with fury, his bloodshot eyes fixed on the boys, Brynjar reached down and grabbed his helmet. Frankie watched him, his mouth dry. Maybe now that Brynjar had his helmet back, he'd calm down a bit?

But that is not what happened. Not at all. As Brynjar lifted the helmet, it tipped to one side and out rolled three little round paintballs: one red, one yellow, one blue.

Brynjar picked up one of the balls, squeezing it until it popped. By the light of the aurora's glow, the yellow paint on his hand was easy to make out.

Brynjar stared at the coloured blotch, then looked over to where the bear's body lay. Frankie could practically SEE him joining the dots in his head.

A great hush fell over the scene. The owls stopped hooting, the crickets stopped chirping and even the waves momentarily seemed to stop crashing against the sand. And in that moment of almost pure silence, Drew clutched Frankie's arm and uttered a single word:

**'RUN!'**

# CHAPTER 10

## YET ANOTHER GREAT ESCAPE

Frankie belted towards the forest, his heart pounding so hard that it felt like it was trying to pop out of his chest. From the way Drew was breathing as he ran along beside him, Frankie could tell he felt much the same. As soon as they were on firmer ground, Drew whipped his blue scooter out of his backpack and scooted along instead.

'I'm sorry, I'm sorry!' Drew yelled again as they raced away. 'I was only going to borrow it!'

Frankie was huffing and puffing like a steam train with asthma, but even as the yelling died down in the distance, he knew they weren't out of trouble yet.

From the sound of the thumping behind them, they were being followed – by something large and scary.

'Oh great, another bear,' Frankie moaned, jumping over a bush. 'That's just what we need right now.'

But when he heard a whinnying sound, he realised that someone was chasing after them on horseback ... and that he was probably about to be caught.

'Keep going!' he screamed to Drew, who was up ahead on his scooter. The words had only just left his mouth as he felt a hand grab him by the collar and lift him into the air.

Feeling like his remaining living moments were now definitely in the single digits, Frankie squeezed his eyes shut.

But rather than hearing the **swish** of an axe-blade heading towards him, Frankie found himself being tossed onto the back of the galloping horse. He opened one eye cautiously. Then the other. A huge grin spread across his face when he saw who was riding the horse. It was Birger!

Frankie had never felt more relieved. Birger called out something that Frankie figured probably meant, 'Hold on!' and he did just that. He held on to Birger as tightly as a mouse in a cyclone holding onto the last piece of cheese in town.

Drew Bird, who had whipped up some serious speed on his blue scooter, led the way back to the gnarled tree (which seemed to look more like Grandad every time Frankie saw it), where the group finally slowed to a stop.

Birger dismounted from his noble steed in a single, effortless movement, but Frankie wished he had a ladder to get off the huge horse. He slithered down cautiously and was extremely happy when his feet finally hit the ground. He turned to see Drew standing in front of Birger.

'Birger,' said Drew, looking shame-faced. 'I'm so sorry about the Viking helmet. I thought no-one would mind if I borrowed it for a bit, because it was so old and scuffed up.'

'Brynjar is very proud of his helmet,' Birger explained, once the padlock had done its translation. 'Our father gave it to him.'

'Oops,' said Drew guiltily. 'Sorry. I didn't know.'

Birger smiled. 'It was a mistake. Everyone makes them,' he said. Then his smile faded. 'Except my brother. Everything **he** does is **perfect.**'

'My big sister is like that,' Frankie said, sympathetically.

'Your sister is good at wielding an axe too?' Birger queried. 'And she is the village arm-wrestling champion? And she has the best beard?'

'Well, no,' admitted Frankie. 'But she always gets straight As and she **never** burps at the table. It's hard to live up to her standards.' Frankie felt extremely sorry for Birger. And his guilty conscience about his own role in Birger's father's death was weighing on him heavily.

Maybe he and Drew should just tell Birger what they'd done to the bear. Or maybe Drew was right, and they should go back in time to undo their mistake ...

Drew tapped Frankie on the shoulder. 'Um, sorry to break this up, but we should go,' he said. 'I think I can hear someone coming.'

Frankie nodded. If Brynjar was on his way, it was definitely time to go. But then his insides **lurched** as he remembered something. 'I don't have time to set up the protective force field, and we've lost Grandad's extra-long belt!' he exclaimed. 'How are we going to form the Circle of Safety?'

Drew grinned. 'Already thought of that. There are heaps of stones lying around here. We can make the circle out of them.'

'Will that work?' Frankie said doubtfully. 'Grandad said there couldn't be any breaks in the circle. It'd be better if we used a scarf or a skipping rope.'

Drew rolled his eyes. 'Somehow I don't think we're going to find those things in a forest in the middle of the Viking era,' he pointed out. 'What we have are rocks. They'll have to do. Let's do this – and fast.'

As Frankie didn't have a better plan, he set to work helping Drew, with Birger watching on curiously. The boys worked as fast as they could, knowing at any moment Brynjar might appear. When they were finished, Drew grabbed the suitcase, the boys stepped into the circle and Frankie began rattling off a hurried farewell to Birger.

'As much as we would love to hang out with you,' he said, 'we have a very important Halloween Parade to –'

But his words were cut short by a loud rumbling noise that rolled through the woods. It sounded like thunder but much more scary. Even worse, it was growing **louder** by the second. Their hearts thumping with terror, Frankie and

Drew turned to see the one person they didn't want to see right then (and no, it wasn't one of the Mosley triplets or Lisa Chadwick).

It was, of course, a raging Brynjar – his anger red hot and visible even from approximately one hundred metres away.

He spotted the terrified group and ***ROARED*** as he charged towards them, pushing his way between trees and leaping over boulders.

Frankie flung open the suitcase and rainbow-coloured light poured out. With trembling hands, he mashed in the co-ordinates. He could smell Brynjar, could *feel* him hurtling towards them, only seconds away.

He heard a huge scream as Brynjar launched himself into the air and towards the stone circle. Then there was another roar as Birger also leapt up, like an AFL footballer taking a mark, colliding with his brother and pushing him away just in the nick of time.

Brynjar fell to the ground a metre or so away, but Birger fell *inside* the stone circle, groaning as he clutched his head.

'We have to get him out of here,' said Drew, desperately trying to push the huge Viking teenager out of the circle.

With a groan, Brynjar began staggering to his feet. Not knowing what else to do, Frankie swung the open suitcase around to face him, hoping to dazzle Brynjar long enough for them to make their escape. Brynjar looked at the colours and whirling things inside the suitcase, his eyes wide.

'I can't shift Birger,' yelled Drew.

Now, not all ideas are equal. There are brilliant ideas and very, very **stupid ideas**. The idea that came to Frankie fell somewhere near the middle, although somewhat closer to the stupid idea side. But desperate times call for desperate measures, and Brynjar had just stopped looking at the suitcase and started shaking his fist at Frankie and Drew instead ...

'We'll have to take Birger with us!' Frankie shouted.

'Are you sure that's a good idea?' Drew gasped.

'I'm positive it's *not*, but we have no choice!' Frankie flung back, screwing his eyes shut and pressing the final button on the suitcase's dashboard. 'Happy travels, I guess –'

And the boys disappeared from the forest ... before anyone could notice that in all the chaos, one of the white stones in the Circle of Safety had been knocked out of place.

# CHAPTER 11

# THE SHED IS FORBIDDEN AGAIN

Imagine being stretched.

Stretched over time and distance and music and space. Stretched like a slingshot pulled back by a giant's hand, but not knowing if you are facing forwards or backwards, so that as the giant releases the shot you cannot be sure if you are travelling up or down or sideways.

Abraham Lincoln eats pizza as Steve Irwin gets tickled by a crocodile giggling like a three-year-old on Christmas morning. Achilles has his ankles strapped by Arthur Conan Doyle.

Marilyn Monroe dances with Weary Dunlop as a World War II army tank shoots fireworks into outer space.

In time travel, nothing makes **sense,** but somehow, nothing feels like **nonsense** either.

Drew tried to scream at Frankie but the only things that came out of his mouth were bubbles.

Frankie was just able to make out a spinning ant below his feet. It wasn't really a spinning ant, though. It was actually planet Earth and Frankie, Drew and Birger were hurtling towards it at the speed of sound.

And before they could say, 'Hold on,' the boys were back at home. Well, they were in Grandad Fish's backyard, actually. To be even more precise, Drew was hanging upside down from the apple tree and Frankie had landed smack bang in the compost heap. Birger, who was out cold, was stretched beneath the Hills hoist, his head resting on Nanna Fish's peg bucket. Frankie and Drew took a few moments to get themselves together. They weren't just in a state of shock – they were in an entire *country* of shock.

Which isn't so surprising. Only seconds earlier they were about to be hit by a raging Brynjar and now they were sitting in a suburban backyard in the late afternoon with a couple of garden gnomes and an unconscious Viking. Neither of the boys had any idea what to do next. And then Birger began to stir.

'What should we do?' Drew asked, his eyes round. 'Take him back before he wakes up fully?'

Frankie considered this option, then shook his head. 'No, Brynjar might be there waiting for us. And besides, the Sonic Suitcase needs to be recharged. And the padlock's come off.' The charge level on the suitcase's display read **17 per cent**. He looked over at the shed and saw a crack of light shining through the curtains.

'I'll go and talk to Grandad about it,' Frankie decided.

Grandad was definitely the family member who was least likely to freak out about Frankie turning up on his doorstep with a **ViKing**. On the other hand, Frankie wasn't sure how Grandad would react when he heard that Frankie and Drew's actions had led to the death of someone in history, even though it *had* been an accident.

The bad feeling about what had happened was still lodged in the pit of Frankie's stomach. Drew seemed to sense his nervousness. 'I'll come with you,' he offered.

But even as Drew spoke, his phone began to beep furiously from within his backpack as a backlog of messages began downloading (there's no phone reception in time travel – not yet, anyway).

Drew fished it out and groaned. 'Seventy-three messages from Mum, and counting,' he reported. 'She must have been trying to reach me while we were away.' With a regretful sigh, Drew stood up. 'I'd better go. She'll freak if I don't make it home in time for dinner.'

Frankie nodded. 'Sure. Call me later?'

Drew grinned. 'You bet!' Then he added, 'I really am **sorry** about the helmet, Frankie. I was just borrowing it. I didn't mean to cause all that trouble.'

As Drew hurried away, Birger started to sit up, rubbing his head and looking around in complete bewilderment. It was lucky that he seemed to be a 'take it all in his stride' kind of Viking, Frankie reflected. All the same, Frankie thought it best if he kept him out of Grandad's sight, at least initially.

'Stay here ... just for a moment,' Frankie instructed him, leading Birger over to Nanna's exquisite flowerbeds and praying he wouldn't stomp all over her forget-me-nots. The padlock in his hand didn't make a sound, but Birger seemed to understand, so Frankie scooted over to the Forbidden Shed – only to find the door was locked.

**Thud! Thud! Thud!** went Frankie's fists on the old wooden door. No-one answered. Frankie pressed his ear against the wooden planks. He could definitely hear murmurings inside – it sounded like two people were in there. He recognised Grandad's gravelly tones straight away. And then Frankie froze. The other voice was female ... and it definitely wasn't Nanna.

'Grandad! Are you in there?' Frankie bellowed.

The murmurings abruptly stopped and Frankie heard someone walking cautiously across the squeaky floorboards. Then the door opened a crack and Grandad's head appeared.

'What do ye want, kiddo?' Grandad snapped. He seemed flustered, and not particularly happy to see Frankie.

'Can I come in?' asked Frankie urgently.

'Um ...' said Grandad, nervously looking back over his shoulder into the Forbidden Shed. 'No. Not now. I want to have a chat with ye soon, but not right now, OK?'

'But I've got to charge the suitcase!' wailed Frankie.

Grandad's right hook shot out, grabbed the suitcase and pulled it into the Forbidden Shed. The door shut with a **bang**.

Frankie began thumping on the door again.

'Grandad, is someone in there with you?' he called. 'I need your help with something. It's important!'

But there was no answer.

Briefly, Frankie considered asking Nanna Fish if he and Birger could stay with them. But then he remembered it was Friday – the night Nanna held her *Family Feud* Fan Club meeting. There was no way he could bring a teenage Viking into Nanna's house when all her friends were there, shouting at the TV!

Frankie walked despondently back to Birger, who was keeping a careful eye on a moth that was fluttering around his nose.

'Well, Birger. It looks like you're staying at my house tonight,' said Frankie.

Birger just looked straight back at Frankie, puzzled. The padlock in his hand seemed to have been damaged in the landing and was – hopefully only temporarily – not working.

*Typical!* Frankie thought grumpily. It felt like

his problems just kept getting **bigger** and more complicated.

What Frankie didn't realise was that his problems were actually *way bigger* and far *more* complicated than he could even imagine. Because, shortly after he led an extremely curious Birger home through the side gate, another figure woke up, tucked away out of sight behind the (once again) Forbidden Shed.

Confused, **dizzy** and disoriented, the figure sat up and looked around, trying to work out where he was. He seemed to be wedged behind some kind of small wooden building, not completely dissimilar to the one he himself lived in roughly nine hundred years in the past. But he was quite sure this was *not* his house and that somehow he'd ended up very far away from home.

Brynjar frowned. This was the fault of those strange thieving boys, he was sure of it. He staggered to his feet.

'Birger?' he called, a little worried. Then, getting no reply, he grabbed his axe and stomped out towards the street ...

# CHAPTER 12

# VALHALLA OR RUMPUS ROOM?

Historically, Frankie's parents – Ron and Tina Fish – had not been particularly keen on sleepovers, particularly in recent times as they worked around the clock to keep their business, Fish Pest Control, running. The last thing they wanted when they finally got home in the evening was extra kids in the house.

But Frankie was fast running out of options. He had considered taking Birger to Drew's house, but Gary Bird had very sharp eyes and would surely notice a giant Norse teenager in his living room. And anyway, Frankie's parents were far less observant. The stress of their new business meant they weren't always completely aware of what was going on in their children's lives.

Frankie was pretty sure Ron Fish had hastily wrapped up a set of playing cards for his eleventh birthday only *after* he'd found the huge sign Frankie had taped to the toilet door that said, 'Tomorrow is Frankie's Birthday'. On the same day, Tina Fish had presented him with a 'birthday cake' that was simply a Wagon Wheel with a single candle stuck on top with Blu Tack.

Yep, that birthday kind of **sucked**.

BUT, on the bright side ... his mum and dad barely noticed when Frankie got a D in Geography last year, or that Frankie often stayed up late watching the **bottle-flipping championships** – the Flippies – on YouTube.

So there was a good chance Ron and Tina Fish wouldn't be aware that a strange bearded boy dressed like, well, a Viking, was camping out in their house. At least, Frankie hoped so.

'This is where I live,' Frankie announced to a still bewildered Birger after they had miraculously managed to make it to the Fish house incognito. He opened the front door and led Birger downstairs, to the rumpus room – the rather neglected space where he had once spent hours playing as a kid. Ron and Tina Fish had long ago declared it a kids-only area (possibly so they didn't have to deal with the hassle of renovating it into something more modern), which made it the best place in the house to hide Birger. So long as Birger stayed in there, things would be fine.

'And this is the rumpus room,' said Frankie, gesturing to various things in the room. 'It's got a table-tennis table, bean bags, a TV ...'

Birger walked slowly towards the blank TV screen. *What is this strange little box?* Frankie imagined Birger thinking to himself.

To be fair, even Frankie thought the TV was weird. Ron Fish took his time updating technology, hence the bulky, box-like old telly and the ancient VCR that sat beneath it. (Being in the rumpus room was a bit like being stuck in a 1990s time warp – one you didn't need a time machine to get to.)

'You don't seem to be freaking out about all of this as much as I thought you might,' Frankie mused.

Birger pointed around at the room. 'Valhalla? Birger ... in ... Valhalla?'

'Um ...' came the less-than-helpful response from Frankie Fish, Professional Tour Guide for the Historically Misplaced.

Frankie only knew little bits of Viking mythology, mostly gleaned from the *Thor* movies and that one documentary he'd seen with his dad. He remembered, however, that Valhalla was where Vikings hoped to go when they died, sort of like heaven.

It was a tricky question for Frankie to answer.

On one hand, saying 'yes' would explain the transition of worlds that Birger had just experienced in a way that he would understand. On the other, it would lead Birger to believe he was dead.

This is not the kind of dilemma that a twelve-year-old should have to deal with but then again, most twelve-year-olds are not time travellers (please contact the publisher if you are aware of any).

'No, not Valhalla,' Frankie heard his mouth saying, without waiting for permission from his brain. 'Rumpus room.'

'Rumpus *røm*,' Birger repeated slowly, nodding his head with reverence like he was inside a holy church.

'That's right,' Frankie confirmed, impressed that Birger was already picking up some English, especially as the padlock still seemed to be on the blink. As Birger tentatively touched the worn-out old couch, Frankie heard the phone ringing upstairs. 'Stay here,' he said, and bolted off to answer it.

It was Drew. 'What's happening?' he said enthusiastically. 'Is Birger still here?'

'Yes, he's in my rumpus room,' Frankie replied, barely believing the words floating out of his mouth.

'No. WAY!' Drew screamed with laughter.

'Well, it's only for tonight hopefully, just until the Sonic Suitcase recharges ...'

'Did you see your grandad?' Drew asked, his curiosity practically dripping through the phone. 'Did you find out if he really does have a girlfriend?'

'He was definitely acting **weird**,' Frankie admitted.

'I think all old people act weird,' said Drew reassuringly. 'It's like they get to a certain age and say to themselves, "I'm going to be weird now. I'm going to wear my dressing gown to the movies and grow a beard like a wizard." Or, in your grandad's case, "I'm going to **build a time machine** and get a secret girlfriend",' Drew chuckled.

'I guess,' said Frankie, who really didn't want to contemplate what was going on with his grandad right now. 'Hey, wanna come over for a sleepover?' He could practically hear Drew's grin on the other end of the line.

'Duh! I'll be there faster than you can say *dorky dad fashion*.'

Frankie knew that ever since last semester's school assembly prank, when he and Drew had unfurled a fake banner that had led to **all kinds of trouble**, Drew Bird wasn't exactly his mum and dad's favourite person. But if they didn't notice the Viking kid in the rumpus room then they probably wouldn't notice Drew Bird either. At least, that was what Frankie was banking on ...

# CHAPTER 13

## SLEEPOVER WITH A VIKING

Ron and Tina Fish were absolutely pooped when they got home after a hectic day of removing wasp nests and wiping up mouse-plague poo.

They were greatly relieved (and more than a little surprised) when Frankie informed them he had made himself dinner. Tina kissed him on the forehead. Then she frowned.

'Did you hear something just then? It sounded like it was coming from the rumpus room.

A sort of ... **thumping**, shuffling, moving around sound.'

Frankie coughed nervously.

Ron groaned. 'Don't tell me we've got some kind of pest in our own house,' he said. 'I suppose I'd better go and have a look.'

**'No, don't!'** Frankie said, a bit too loudly. His dad gave him a curious look. 'Um ... it's just ...' Desperately, Frankie tried to think of something, anything, to tell his parents that would keep them away from the rumpus room. 'I've been making a Halloween costume down there,' he said. 'I had to ... er... move some boxes around. One of them must have fallen over, that's all.'

There was another thump, followed by a shout.

Frankie felt all the blood drain from his face. 'That's just the telly,' he said hurriedly, ushering his parents away from the rumpus room stairs. 'I was ... um ... watching a show about Vikings.

While I was making my costume. I better hurry back and finish it, the parade's tomorrow!'

'Oh, I'd forgotten about that,' Tina said, stifling a yawn. 'Can I see it?'

**'NO!'** Frankie shouted. 'I mean ... er ... no. It's going to be a surprise! Why don't you and Dad have an early night instead?'

'OK ...' said Tina, already heading down the hall. Ron followed her, and Frankie heaved a huge sigh of relief. But Ron had only been gone a moment when he stopped and turned around.

'Hey, Frankie,' he said.

Frankie swallowed nervously. What if his dad insisted on checking the rumpus room for pests? 'Yes?'

'I've been pretty busy lately, haven't I? How about we have a day soon where we just hang out together. We could kick the footy or see that new superhero movie?'

Frankie nodded. 'That'd be great!' he said, feeling both very relieved and very happy.

But almost immediately, his good feeling was replaced by a bad one. Birger and Brynjar no longer *had* a father to do whatever activities it was that Vikings did with their dads.

Frankie forced a smile at his dad, and tried to squash the thought down. Right now, he had to concentrate on keeping Birger out of sight and getting him back home.

Once the coast was clear, Frankie sneaked down the hallway to the kitchen. On the way, he caught Saint Lou sneaking in the front door. Frankie was pretty sure Lou had basketball training on Fridays, but Lou wasn't wearing her sports gear. So where had she been? And why did she look so guilty?

Their conversation went like this:

'What have you been doing?' Frankie asked suspiciously.

'Nothing. Why?' Lou replied, more than a little defensively. 'And why are you talking to me? You never talk to me.'

'Well, I thought I'd start now,' said Frankie smoothly. The more rattled his sister looked, the more his curiosity was piqued. He heard another thump from the rumpus room and spoke a bit louder to try to cover the sound. 'Tell me, **saint sissy sis**, what are you dressing up as for the Halloween Parade tomorrow?'

'Don't call me that,' said Lou, trying to edge away from Frankie and towards her room. 'And anyway, I'm not entering this year.'

'*Not entering?*' Frankie couldn't believe his ears. Right then he wouldn't have believed them even if they'd just won the Nobel Prize for Most Trustworthy Ears in the World. Lou *always* entered and, if he were being completely honest, her costumes were even better than Lisa Chadwick's (not that this would make any difference while Mrs Chadwick was the lead judge). 'Why not?'

Lou went red and she coughed. 'I … I've got a lot going on right now.'

Frankie looked at his sister through narrowed eyes. Unbelievable as it was, he strongly suspected she had a boyfriend. But before he could cross-examine her on this topic, Lou squeezed past him and rushed off down the hall.

'Well-I'm-pooped-going-to-bed-nighty-night!' she said, and slammed the door.

It was possibly the longest conversation Frankie had had with his sister in months – and definitely the strangest. He smirked to himself, pretty sure that his boyfriend theory was right. He immediately looked forward to teasing his sister about it for many days/weeks/months/years to come.

Now that he was finally alone again, Frankie completed his raid on the kitchen, heading back to the rumpus room armed with chips, cookies, milk, juice and ice-cream (maybe this was a version of Valhalla, after all).

'What were all those thumping noises?' he asked Drew.

'Birger was showing me some more dance steps,' Drew replied from where he was now sprawled out on the couch.

'Well, we'll have to do something quieter with him for the rest of the night,' Frankie replied. 'My parents and Saint Lou are upstairs now and we can't risk them hearing him.'

'Can we show him TV?' Drew begged, grabbing a fistful of chocolate-chip cookies and tossing them into his excited gob. 'Please, please, pretty please!'

Frankie thought about it. They had worked really hard to keep the details of the modern world from Ping during their last adventure, when they had had to bring her all the way from Imperial China to the present day so she could have life-saving surgery. But Birger had already seen so much of the modern world that Frankie didn't think it would matter if he saw a little more. 'OK,' he said, picking up the remote.

**CLICK**.

And with that, Frankie and Drew lost Birger for the next few hours. He was experiencing his own time-travelling machine and was absolutely enthralled by it.

Frankie felt both nervous and thrilled by Birger's reaction. It was obvious he was seeing things he'd never even dreamt of before, including an ad that showed several people dressed as Vikings, who were all wearing horned hats. Birger roared with laughter when he saw that, and the boys didn't need the padlock translator to tell them Birger was saying real Viking helmets didn't have horns.

'So, when do we send him back?' said Drew

when the laughter had died down.

'Tomorrow, if we can get him out of the house without my parents seeing him first. And if Grandad will let us use the Sonic Suitcase,' Frankie said. 'Because Qantas doesn't fly to the Viking era.'

'Oh, thanks a lot, Captain Obvious. Is the Earth round too?' retorted Drew. 'So, what are we going to do about the Halloween Parade? We've only got one helmet so far.'

With a yawn, Frankie took a handful of chips and flopped down into a beanbag. 'We can figure out the rest of our costumes once we've got Birger home,' he said. *And once I've worked out what do to about his dad that won't destroy the timeline or muck up history,* he thought to himself. *No biggie ...*

Frankie spent the rest of the night thinking it through. But before he could figure it out, he was asleep.

# CHAPTER 14

# BAD NEWS

When Frankie Fish woke up late on Saturday morning, he went from bleary-eyed to wide-eyed within seconds.

That's what happens when you suddenly remember you have a Viking sleeping in your rumpus room on **HALLOWEEN** without your parents (or sister) knowing.

Frankie leapt up and bounded upstairs so he could get things ready in the Fish kitchen well before his parents arrived at the breakfast table.

When they finally staggered in, Frankie beamed at them like the cover child from *Perfect Child Weekly*. 'Morning, Mum. Morning, Dad!'

'Morning, son,' they both groaned, sounding like teenagers that had been woken two hundred years too early.

'I've made you some toast and juice,' Frankie announced, hoping this would speed up his parents' exit from the house (Tina and Ron worked every day of the week, *including* Saturdays). He had even put the toast in a little paper bag and the juice in two of Saint Lou's many eco-friendly reusable cups.

'Oh, what a golden child,' glowed Tina Fish, accepting her bag of toast.

Ron Fish was equally impressed, and smiled at his son proudly. 'You've certainly pulled up your socks since that banner proposal prank, Frankie-boy. Looks like spending more time with your grandparents has got you back on the straight and narrow.'

Tina Fish – also known as Tuna Fish – checked her watch, then smiled at Frankie's dad. 'Are we really in such a rush this morning, love? With this kind of service maybe we should eat in today.'

'I was thinking the same thing,' enthused Ron. 'A table for two, please!' he joked, clicking his fingers at Frankie.

'Oh no, we are strictly takeaway only,' Frankie half-joked back. He was starting to feel nervous.

'Do you do coffee too?' enquired Tina Fish.

'Um, well ...'

Frankie was just about to improvise a pathetic answer when Saint Lou blew in like a storm in desperate need of making a splash.

'Mum and Dad, you should leave right now! Traffic is **crazy**. I just saw on the news that there's some enormous nutter with a red beard shouting **gibberish** on a **rampage** around the city.'

Frankie felt a frog do a triple-twist dive into

his throat in pike position.

**GULP.**

'How was he dressed?' he asked nervously.

'Kind of like a Viking,' said Lou, 'but without the horned hat.'

Frankie scowled. 'Vikings didn't *have* –'

But Lou had already turned back to her parents. 'Seriously, guys. You should take that toast for the road.'

'The world is getting crazier, no doubt about it,' replied Ron Fish, forgoing his relaxed breakfast with a sigh. 'Let's get going, Tina love.'

Frankie's head was spinning faster than the winning contestant in a *Make Yourself Dizzy* contest.

*The rampaging Viking can't be Birger*, he thought as his Mum kissed him on the cheek and thanked him for the 'very thoughtful breakfast'. So who was it then? He had an **awful feeling** he knew the answer.

The moment they were gone, Frankie dashed

back to the rumpus room. Drew and Birger were doing *Just Dance* on the Xbox. Birger looked like he had never had so much fun in his entire life.

'Put the news on!' Frankie demanded.

'But news is boring,' moaned Drew.

'Just do it!' shouted Frankie, like he was providing the voice-over for the last Nike commercial on earth.

Drew, finally realising something serious was up, quickly grappled with the remote and switched it to the news.

A man with perfect hair and perfect teeth was speaking.

*'The city is at a standstill this morning as Halloween fever hits early. One keen Halloweener has gone to great lengths to dress up as a Viking and I have to say he looks extremely authentic, except that he's missing the horned hat –'*

'Vikings didn't wear horned hats, you idiot!' Drew snapped at the screen. But Frankie was too amazed by the footage of the Viking to say a word. He stared at the TV with eyes larger than a Shrove Tuesday pancake.

There on the screen was Brynjar, running down the main street of town, yelling out what sounded like **extremely rude words** in Ancient Norse.

Frankie felt his whole body go cold. *How on earth did he –*

But it didn't matter *how* Brynjar had got there. How on earth were they going to get him *back* where he belonged?

Mr Perfect reappeared on the screen.

*'We have our reporter down in the City Square and I believe she is about to attempt to talk with this so-called Viking man ... Over to you, Gertrude Cross, live in the city.'*

The reporter appeared.

*'Yes Ross, Halloween certainly started with a "roar" today. Firstly I must correct you because, despite the impressive beard, the troublemaker appears in fact to be a teenager and not an adult and*

*I have to say he seems to have gone to extraordinary lengths to create his costume. He even smells how I imagine Vikings may smell, like a fart trapped in a rotting fish. He's just over there and so I'm going to try to speak to him. Perhaps we can discover why his helmet is missing horns!'*

'BECAUSE VIKINGS ...' Drew started to yell, then slumped back into his seat, looking defeated. 'Ah, forget it,' he muttered.

Gertrude approached a confused-looking Brynjar, who was surrounded by excited tourists taking selfies with him.

*'Excuse me,'* Gertrude said with a smile so toothy it would make a piranha jealous. *'I must congratulate you on your incredible costume. Where did you get it from?'*

Brynjar looked down the barrel of the camera and simply said, *'Birger.'*

*'Oh, I've heard of Birger!*
*It's one of those fancy new European department stores, isn't it? Very swish. So, where have you come from today?'*

'BIRGER.'

*'OK, so you've come straight from the store. I too like to show off my clothes as soon as I buy them. And how will you be spending your Halloween tonight?'*

Brynjar was clearly becoming more and more frustrated. His chest heaved as he screamed loudly into Gertrude's microphone, spittle flying from his mouth.

**'BIRRRRGERRRRRR!'**

Everyone stopped what they were doing and stared at him in alarm, then moved aside as Brynjar took off through the crowd.

*'Back to you in the studio, Ross,'* reported a slightly shocked and spittle-covered Gertrude Cross.

Meanwhile, back in the Fish household, that frog in Frankie's throat had swelled to the size of a crocodile.

# CHAPTER 15

## GRANDAD, WE HAVE A PROBLEM

The one thing you can count on with old people is that they will always be home. And sure enough, when Frankie, Drew and a Viking named Birger turned up that Saturday morning – the day of the Halloween Parade – Alfie and Mavis Fish were already onto their fourth cup of tea for the morning.

'Grandad, we have a problem,' Frankie said, cutting to the chase, as soon as he emerged from a Nanna Fish cuddle.

*'We?'* retorted Grandad. 'I think ye mean *ye*. I have no problem.'

Frankie sighed. 'OK then, *I* have a problem. But if you don't help *me* it'll be everybody's problem very soon.'

'Don't torture the boy, Alfred,' tutted Nanna Fish. 'Listen to what he has to say.'

Luckily for Frankie, Nanna Fish was the one person Grandad actually paid attention to.

'OK, kiddo,' he said. 'What do ye need from me?'

'I need the Sonic Suitcase back.'

'Oh, what a surprise, I had no idea it was going to involve *that* at all,' Grandad replied, sarcasm draped over every word. 'And tell me. Who is your silent bearded friend here? I'm guessing he's not an exchange student, is he?'

All eyes landed on Birger, who was quietly taking up most of the couch in one of Frankie's dad's polo shirts (which Frankie had nicked from the ironing basket to help him blend in).

'It wouldn't have been a complete lie,' Drew interjected. 'He *is* from Norway.'

'Go on,' Grandad said, his eyes narrowing.

'Just from about nine hundred years ago ...'

Grandad's nostrils **flared** a little, like those of a bull that has just spotted something fluttering and red.

'Birger is a Viking,' Frankie stammered. 'And we accidentally brought him back with us.'

Grandad buried his head in his hands, then rubbed his face like he was trying to get paint off it. 'How many times have we been through this? We are time travellers, not time meddlers. When ye meddle with time, ye **mess with time**. **YE TAUGHT ME THAT, FRANCIS**.'

Frankie gulped.

'Would your Viking friend like a cup of tea?' asked Nanna Fish politely. But no-one was listening.

'I can explain,' said Frankie, desperately.

‘We went back in time to Norway to borrow some Viking clothes –’

Grandad thumped the coffee table, making the tea cups jump. ‘Why on earth did ye want to borrow Viking clothes?’ he **roared**. His face was purple.

‘I gave you a lovely hand-knitted jumper for Christmas, dear,’ Nanna reminded him, handing a cup of tea to Birger. ‘And I can always knit you another, any time of year!

No need to go borrowing Viking clothes.'

'We wanted to win the Best Costume prize at Lisa Chadwick's Halloween Parade,' Frankie muttered. 'And we just got excited.'

'A little too excited, obviously,' Drew explained forlornly, and then added, 'it's my first Halloween Parade at St Monica's.'

Grandad was ready to reload and yell again, but then he looked at Drew, who now had his head bowed, and then at Frankie.

'Did ye not use the Circle of Safety?' Grandad groaned. 'It was supposed to prevent mistakes like this.'

'We *did* use it!' protested Frankie. 'But we, er, lost the belt. And something went wrong with it anyway ...'

Grandad got to his feet and paced around the kitchen, rubbing the back of his head. 'I guess I am a little bit to blame here,' he muttered. 'I mean, I did invent a time machine and what's the point of having a time machine if you're not going to use it?'

'That's right!' Frankie said, leaping on Grandad's sentiment like a frog leaping onto a cake made of flies.

'And it's not every day ye get a real Viking sitting in yer lounge,' Grandad said, glaring at Birger, who was staring with interest at Nanna as she sipped from the tiny floral tea cup.

'I know, right?' said Drew, enthusiastically. 'When you think about it, it is **pretty cool**.'

'So, ye need the Sonic Suitcase to return him to his Viking family in Norway?' growled Grandad.

'Well, Birger is not actually our biggest problem right now,' Frankie admitted nervously.

Grandad turned and stared at him. 'What *is* your biggest problem then?'

Frankie suddenly felt **hot** and **sweaty**.

'Um ... have you seen the news this morning by any chance?'

Grandad looked at Frankie for a moment, then dashed over to the TV and clicked it on.

'Are we watching *Family Feud?*' Nanna asked hopefully.

'Um, kind of,' said Frankie. Even at a moment of great stress, he couldn't resist making fun of her love for *Family Feud*. But his smirk quickly fell away when a close-up of a **furious** bearded face filled the screen.

'Brynjar,' Birger whispered, walking towards the TV and gently touching the screen.

The news was cycling through various clips of Brynjar, whom everyone seemed to be treating as either a joke or a publicity stunt. Some of the clips were of Brynjar looking angry, others showed him looking confused and posing for selfies with tourists. No-one seemed to know what to make of him. Was he **crazy** or was he part of some **Halloween stunt**?

The only people who truly understood the severity of what was going on were currently huddled around Grandad's twenty-year-old TV. Finally, the old man coughed and uttered what was probably the most obvious statement ever made in the history of obvious statements.

'Right. Looks like ye've really **screwed up** this time, lad.'

# CHAPTER 16

# THE SEARCH FOR BRYNJAR

In their extremely short (but still way too long) time spent with the Vikings, Frankie had realised that the best strategy for survival was to stay away from Brynjar. Brynjar was angry, prone to yelling and had breath like he had swallowed a big fish that had drowned in garlic.

For all these reasons, running **AWAY** from Brynjar was highly recommended. Running **TOWARDS** him, as they now planned to do, seemed like a very foolish idea.

Double **YIKES** in pike position.

Frankie ran through his current 'to do' list: hunt down a furious Viking, then send him and his Viking brother back home before the world found out what was going on and utter chaos was unleashed. There was also the small matter of Lisa Chadwick's Halloween Parade, which was now only a few hours away.

Somehow, even after everything that had happened, Frankie found himself hoping madly that they'd still be able to compete and win that hundred-dollar Cocoa Pit voucher once and for all. But it wasn't looking likely ...

Judging by what they'd seen on the TV news, it looked like Brynjar was probably heading towards the city's Botanic Gardens. Since Grandad had lost his licence, a train ride was required to get there – as soon as possible.

Can you imagine a flying Whattsiedonk? Or a hovering Hopposwank?

Probably not.

Don't feel sad. The reason you cannot fathom a Whattsiedonk or a Hopposwank is because they have not been invented (and let's face it, probably never will be).

So you can imagine how confused and amazed Birger was as he rode on a train with Frankie, Drew and Grandad that day. Not only was he sitting inside what appeared to him to be a great steel serpent, it was moving. Fast.

'His head might **explode** from sensory overload, if we are not careful,' Grandad said, concerned. With the Sonic Suitcase on his lap – and the translator padlock once again clipped to its handle – Grandad was keeping a sharp eye on Birger, who stared out at the world **whizzing past** in fascination.

Frankie had to admit that Grandad had a very good point. The smells, the colours, the machines – Birger was experiencing a whole new world and Frankie wasn't sure how they could get him to forget it all. It would be like trying to forget the first time you saw fireworks or went on an aeroplane.

In other words: **basically impossible**.

As the train pulled to a stop at the station nearest the Botanic Gardens, Drew asked a very good question, particularly by Drew's standards. 'How exactly are we going to catch Brynjar?'

'I have no idea,' admitted Frankie. 'Any suggestions?'

Instantly, Drew outlined three bird-brained ones. They were:

1. Taser him, put him in a wheelbarrow and wheel him home.

2. Use a Wonder Woman-style golden lasso to rope him up. (It was Drew's favourite superhero movie after *Thor: Ragnarok*.)

3. Ask him really, really nicely to come back home with them.

All utterly useless.

Disappointed, Frankie shrugged. 'I guess we'll work it out when we find him.'

'Yeah, because that's worked out so well for us so far,' Drew answered sarcastically, a little offended that Frankie had rejected all of his brilliant ideas.

As the group made its way to the Botanic

Gardens, Frankie and Drew experienced their own **sensory overload**. They had only been to the city a couple of times themselves, and weren't all that familiar with it. Once, they'd come on a school excursion to see the Symphony Orchestra. During the performance, one of the Mosley triplets continuously made fart noises with his armpit. Professional dobber Lisa Chadwick swore some of the noises did not come from his armpit at all.

The class had also come to the city to see a parade and this time another one of the Mosley triplets got in trouble for kicking horse manure in Miss Merryweather's direction. He tried to blame it on the wind, which no-one believed, partly because there was no wind but mostly because there was horse poop all over his shoe.

Drew pulled his blue scooter out of his backpack as Grandad tried to remember which way the Botanic Gardens were. Then they began walking and scooting through the city streets, listening out for a primal Viking scream, their eyes peeled for any signs of Viking destruction.

Surely a Viking as big as Brynjar wouldn't be *too* hard to find ...

Finally, after only three wrong turns and some choice swearwords from Grandad, they arrived at the grand old gates of the Botanic Gardens. *Maybe,* thought Frankie, *this place reminds Brynjar of his homeland?* This green, lush place would have surely looked far more familiar than the grey skyscrapers of the city or the houses out in the suburbs.

Not only were the Botanic Gardens green and lush, they were also **HUGE**. They covered acres and acres. Frankie's heart sank a little as the group walked around the paths, up and down the rolling hills, checking under bushes and up into trees – finding diddly squat.

The place was full of families strolling by, happily chattering about their Halloween costumes and their trick-or-treating plans.

Frankie noticed with a lurch that Birger watched sadly as a father strolled by them, carrying his small son on his shoulders.

'**Oh my carrots!**' Drew Bird screamed suddenly, screeching to a stop on his blue scooter.

Grandad turned around so quickly his head nearly snapped off his neck.

'What the ...?' said Frankie.

'I'm trying to teach Grandad how to swear without swearing,' said Drew.

'No, not that,' Frankie replied, flustered.

Birger simply pointed and stared.

This is what they were all looking at:

The Botanic Gardens included a kids' play area that was full of swings, seesaws, monkey bars and various other pieces of play equipment. With so many fun things to play on, you would think that the kids' play area would be full, but on this occasion it wasn't.

One of the highlights of the kids' play area

was the wooden pirate ship. Kids usually loved climbing aboard, spinning the steering wheel and hoisting the Jolly Roger flag, but today all the kids were staying well clear of it. This was because a strange, huge teenager, dressed like a Viking (but without the horned hat), was standing at the front of the ship, his fist raised in the air, **screaming** in a language that nobody could understand.

Well, *almost* nobody.

# CHAPTER 17

# THE BOY WITH THE SUITCASE

Birger, standing at one end of the kids' play area, stared at his brother in open-mouthed amazement. At that moment, Brynjar stopped shouting and stared back in equally open-mouthed astonishment.

Frankie reached for the padlock on the Sonic Suitcase and turned the key, hoping madly that it was working properly again.

'Birger, do you want to go home?' Frankie asked quickly. The padlock spluttered and crackled, but Frankie heard the word *'heim'*, which sounded like it might mean 'home'.

Birger nodded.

Frankie lifted up the Sonic Suitcase and patted it. 'Well, this is how we get you there.'

Birger frowned. 'It's like ... small longboat?' he asked, via the padlock.

Frankie nodded. 'Yes, like a very small longboat.' Then he pointed to Brynjar. 'You tell him.'

Frankie had no idea if the padlock had done a good job of translating this or not, but Birger went directly over to the base of the wooden pirate ship and began talking earnestly up at his brother, who glared furiously at him.

Drew sidled alongside Frankie. 'How do you think it's going?'

Frankie sighed. 'If I had to guess, I'd say badly.'

There seemed to be a lot of **shouting** and **fist-waving** going on between the Viking brothers.

'Maybe that's just how they always communicate?' suggested Drew.

'If that's the case, then Lou and I have a much better relationship than I realised,' commented Frankie dryly.

Frankie couldn't shake the nasty feeling that Brynjar had guessed the role he and Drew had played in his father's death and was filling Birger in on all the horrible details. The shouting and fist-waving became more intense until suddenly Birger stomped over to Frankie, wrenched the Sonic Suitcase out of his grasp and stomped back towards to his brother.

'Ye let the VIKING take the SUITCASE?' yelled Grandad in horror as Frankie gaped after Birger.

'Bad idea, Frankie, bad idea,' agreed Drew, shaking his head.

'Have *you* ever tried stopping a Viking from getting what he wants?' said Frankie defensively. 'If you're so great, why don't *you* go and get it?'

But before anyone could do anything, Birger

was back at the base of the pirate ship, holding up the suitcase.

If Frankie had been asked to predict how Brynjar would react to this, he'd have guessed that he would:

**A.** Roar.
**B.** Chop up the suitcase with his axe.
**C.** Roar AND chop up the suitcase with his axe.

Which is why the way Brynjar *actually* reacted was such a surprise. He went completely white and backed away from the suitcase so quickly that he almost toppled over the back edge of the pirate ship.

Drew and Frankie stared, their eyes as round as a freshly pumped-up soccer ball.

'Is he ...?' said Drew.

Frankie nodded. 'I think he's *afraid* of the suitcase.'

It seemed so unlikely that a huge, terrifying Viking teenager like Brynjar would be scared of a suitcase, of all things. But every time Birger lifted the suitcase towards him, Brynjar would shriek and recoil in terror. His eyes **bulged** like he was having an allergic reaction and he tried to shield himself from the suitcase as if it were a solar eclipse.

Frankie hurried over to Birger to try to find out what was going on (and hopefully retrieve the suitcase in one piece).

'What's happening, Birger?' Frankie asked anxiously, reaching for the suitcase.

Birger spoke rapidly in reply, gesturing wildly with the suitcase as he did. The padlock did its best to translate.

'Brynjar thinks box ... contains aurora. Very powerful ... aurora can bring good things but also bad ... aurora put colour on bear that killed Father. Brynjar won't go near box ...'

'But that's the only way he can get home!'

AHOY

cried Frankie, frustrated. All the same, he did know how Brynjar felt. It was like the time he denied he had a toothache for a fortnight to avoid going to the dentist.

He rushed over to Grandad and Drew, who were still hanging back from the spectacle.

'What's the deal?' Drew asked immediately.

'Yes, we need to get a wriggle on and get these boys home,' grumbled Grandad.

'Brynjar is petrified of the suitcase,' reported Frankie. 'And now he won't go near it!'

'I don't blame him,' said Grandad. 'It petrifies me too, sometimes.'

Frankie's shoulders slumped. 'I don't know how we can get them home now.'

'Unless ...' Drew Bird said, then stopped, his hands tightening on the handlebars of his electric blue scooter.

'Unless what?' Grandad snapped. 'This is no time for dramatic pauses, lad!'

'Unless ...' Drew continued, stroking his

hairless chin. 'Unless we find something that Brynjar is even MORE frightened of than the suitcase. Then he'll be so scared that he'll *have* to go home just to get away from the thing.'

Frankie had to admit the idea made sense. 'But what?'

'School! Principal Dawson's office! All three Mosley triplets farting at the same time!' quipped Drew Bird.

Grandad quickly squashed the ideas. 'None of that will frighten a Viking, ye numb nut!' he snorted.

Frankie had to admit he was probably right. No, they had to find something **truly terrifying**. Something that would make the suitcase seem like a fluffy bunny rabbit in comparison. He gestured to Birger to come back, and the Viking obliged.

'Is Brynjar *scared* of anything?' Frankie asked him in a low voice. The padlock was making some odd spluttering noises, so Frankie attempted to act out his question to help move things along. He made dramatic shivering gestures like he was cowering from some invisible **evil force**.

'It looks like you're cold,' noted Drew.

'I *don't* look cold,' muttered Frankie, annoyed. 'I look totally scared.'

'Scared of the cold, maybe.'

'I'd like to see how *you* look scared,' Frankie snapped.

'No problem.' Drew took centre stage and cleared his throat, then launched into a dramatic array of movements like he was doing parkour, while also whimpering and pretending to cry.

Birger watched both Frankie's and Drew's performances in astonishment. Then Grandad took his turn to get an answer out of the bewildered Viking, speaking loudly and slowly into the padlock, as if this might help him understand.

'Birger, is your brother afraid of spiders? Ghosts? The dark?' The padlock translated a couple of words haltingly.

'Sharks?' shouted Drew like it was a fun new game. 'Hurricanes? Snakes? Butterflies?'

'Who would be afraid of butterflies?' Grandad snapped.

'My dad is,' Drew insisted. 'He doesn't trust the way they flutter by.'

Birger seemed to finally understand, and his face crumpled a little, as if he were scared of what he was about to say.

*'Draugr,'* he said, trembling.

'Dragor?' Frankie repeated.

'Does he mean "dragons"?' guessed Grandad.

'Maybe Brynjar is scared of Ivan Drago from *Rocky IV*?' asked Drew Bird.

*'Draugr!'* Birger repeated emphatically. Then, as if inspired by Drew's earlier dramatic performance, Birger stuck his arms out in front of him, and lurched around with stiff legs, moaning and groaning. He looked at Frankie meaningfully. *'Draugr!'*

'Did yer Viking mate just swallow a fly?' asked Grandad, concerned.

'Grandad, look the word up on your phone!' said Frankie urgently.

Technically, Grandad had a smart phone, but it was so old that it was more like a 'not-as-smart-as-it-used-to-be' phone. But as neither Drew nor Frankie had brought theirs along (and Birger was several hundred years too old to have one), Grandad's was the only option.

It took him several minutes to get the spelling right and correct his typos ('Why do they make the letters so small on these doaty things?'), but finally the screen in Grandad's hand filled with images.

'What are those **hideous creatures?**' asked Grandad, pulling a face and turning the phone around to show the others.

'They're zombies!' exclaimed Frankie. 'The Viking version.'

'They look like my dad first thing in the

morning,' Drew remarked, a little unkindly.

When Birger saw the pictures, the colour drained from his face and he stumbled backwards. *'Draugr!'* he screamed, dropping the suitcase.

'Are they real?' Drew asked nervously.

'As real as zombies are,' replied Frankie, gulping.

'Try telling your Viking buddy that,' Grandad said. Birger had pulled his cloak out of Drew's backpack and was now cowering beneath it.

Frankie was suddenly feeling a lot more optimistic. 'So we've found our answer then! We'll use *draugr* to scare Brynjar into going back home.'

'Oh sure,' said Grandad with his famous acidic sarcasm as he picked up the suitcase. 'All we need to do is find a mythical creature from the world of the undead and we can send these hairy Vikings back home. Easy-peasy, lemon-squeezy, ye numbskull.'

'What if we told you we could **summon the undead**?' Frankie asked with a twinkle in his eye. Drew grinned too.

'Then I would say yer more deluded than a hitchhiking snake,' Grandad retorted.

'Well, for one night only, we can,' Frankie said. He reached into his pocket and retrieved a piece of paper that he held up for all to see. It read:

Lisa Chadwick's Halloween Parade
and Barbecue Feast
6pm, St Monica's Primary

# CHAPTER 18

## FEAST IS COMING!

To say the stakes were enormous would be like saying the steaks at the local Monster Steak House were a 'decent size'. Lisa Chadwick's Halloween Parade was less than an hour away, and somehow, they had to get Brynjar there without him going crazy again, and hope that the sight of some child-sized zombies marching around would be enough to scare Brynjar all the way home.

As their gang of misfits – two boys, two

hulking Viking teenagers (one of whom was glaring at everyone suspiciously and keeping a firm distance between himself and the suitcase) and a cranky old man – hurried towards St Monica's late that afternoon, Frankie felt like his whole body was tied up in knots.

He decided to ask Grandad about something that had been on his mind since this whole **Viking fiasco** began. Pushing down the nervous lump that had appeared in his throat, he tugged on Grandad's sleeve. 'Hey, can I talk to you for a sec?' he asked in a low voice.

Grandad slowed down his shuffling and raised an eyebrow. 'What is it, lad? We're in kind of a rush here.'

Frankie was mortified when he realised what he was about to say might make him cry. He swallowed, then blurted out: 'Grandad, I think we killed Birger's father.'

Seeing the look of shock on his Grandad's face, Frankie quickly explained what had happened.

'Well, we didn't kill him *ourselves*, but ...'

Grandad listened as the words kept tumbling out of his grandson's mouth, until finally Frankie had to stop. He hadn't taken a breath for about a minute and now he inhaled like a fish waking up from a drowning dream.

Grandad frowned deeply. 'What ye did has probably earned ye a gold medal in this year's *Stupid Move Awards*,' he growled.

Frankie hung his head. 'I know. We made a terrible mistake with that bear, and it changed history. And the worst bit is that I know we can't fix it.' Then he looked up at his grandad, a note of hope creeping into his voice. 'Unless you can think of something we can do? I know it's against the rules, but maybe we can take the Vikings back to just before the bear attack, and … and –'

'No!' Grandad interrupted. 'It's just **not possible**. Think about it, Frankie. If ye returned the Vikings back before they left, there would be doubles – the Viking boys who were there at the time AND the ones ye were returning. Don't ye remember the trouble we got into with all the extra Grandads in Scotland?'

Frankie's stomach dropped like a stone. He *did* remember. And he was in no hurry to repeat the experience.

'I know you're right,' he said miserably. 'I just feel terrible.'

Grandad's face softened a little and he rubbed Frankie's shoulder. 'We time travellers carry a heavy responsibility, lad,' he said. 'I partly blame myself. Ye taught me a lot of these rules, but *I'm* the grown-up. I should never have let ye go off with that **bird-brain** all on yer own. But what's done is done, OK? The best thing now is for ye to get these guys home and not make the same mistake again.'

Frankie nodded, feeling the knots in his tummy loosen ever so slightly. Brynjar and Birger's father was still dead, and Grandad hadn't been able to solve the problem – but he at least seemed to understand. Frankie had been worried he'd be a lot angrier.

They were nearly at the school now, and Drew stopped short. 'Ready to introduce some Vikings to some zombies?' he said quietly to Frankie, his face flushed with excitement.

'By golly I hope this works,' Grandad muttered, shuffling along as fast as he could. 'It will be a disaster if we can't get these Nordic visitors of yers to leave.'

'Oh, I don't know,' reflected Drew. 'It might be fun having a Viking around. He could take us camping.'

'I don't know a lot about Vikings but I know they like to conquer. If these two big lumps of muscle decide to stay, one of them will probably want to be king,' commented Grandad darkly. 'And who knows what they will do to make that happen?'

With a groan, Frankie felt the knots in his tummy tighten right back up. Birger was friendly enough, but he suspected that Brynjar could be pretty vicious. What would happen if he found out he was being led directly into a **trap**?

'We need to move, quick!' commanded Frankie, taking the Sonic Suitcase from Grandad and stepping up his pace.

At that moment, the Viking teens tilted their noses into the sky, closed their eyes and sniffed deeply. At first Frankie had no idea what they were doing. And then Frankie and Drew smelt it too. The unmistakable aroma of barbecue. They were getting close!

Suddenly, a loud, trumpet-like noise burst through the air.

Grandad covered his ears like he had just

accidentally walked into a Foo Fighters concert. 'What in the blazing hell is that?'

Frankie, Drew, Grandad and Birger turned to see Brynjar, standing in the middle of the street, blowing a horn. It was only small but extremely loud.

Evening had begun to fall and lights in the surrounding houses were turning on. Curious neighbours peered out through the curtains to see what was causing what sounded like a medieval car alarm.

'Ssssh!' shooshed Grandad. 'You're ruining the neighbours' dinner!'

'Grandad, it's only five-thirty,' said Frankie, rolling his eyes. 'Believe it or not people do eat later than five-thirty.'

'Well, they shouldn't,' Grandad stated. 'Five-thirty at the latest for me or my digestion goes out the window. What is ye mad Viking mate doing, anyway?'

Brynjar had stopped blowing his horn and

was now looking up towards the stars in the sky above.

'Um ... maybe he's calling a Viking taxi or something?' Drew offered.

'Brynjar gives thanks,' Birger tried to explain through the padlock translator. 'Feast is coming.'

As they hurried along, Frankie noticed there were posters up everywhere for the Halloween Parade. All of them had pictures of Lisa Chadwick in her zombie costumes from previous years – there was one of her dressed as zombiefied Carmen Miranda, and there was another of her as zombiefied Marilyn Monroe – and Frankie found himself grimacing at how **annoying** she was. He wished that ANYONE but her had organised the competition.

But for all of his dislike of Lisa Chadwick Major Events Pty Ltd, Frankie knew that right now this Halloween Parade was their best (and possibly only) chance of getting these Vikings home. He felt a pang of sadness that he and

Drew wouldn't be able to compete this year after all. They had **one Viking helmet** between them, and nothing else.

Then Frankie glanced at Birger, who currently looked less like a Viking and more like a lost puppy – totally confused as to where he was and where he was going. And Frankie remembered that he had a job to do that was way more important than winning a hundred-dollar voucher at the Cocoa Pit.

Plus, no matter how bad Frankie was feeling about the death of Birger's father, he knew that Birger himself must feel much, much worse. He timidly put a hand on the Viking's massive arm and patted it.

'It's OK, Birger. We'll get you both home. **I promise.**'

Now, Frankie Fish had made many promises in his relatively short lifetime.

He'd promised his mum to keep his room tidy. He'd promised his dad to get nothing less than Bs in his tests. He'd promised Saint Lou he'd stop reading her diary when she wasn't home. Sometimes he really meant these things when he said them.

But *this*. This was a promise that he wasn't sure he could keep even as he said it.

Birger smiled. '*Heim ...*' he said, wistfully, and then kept marching on.

'Why don't we send Birger home now and then send Brynjar later – like, when he's fallen asleep or something?' Drew whispered to Frankie.

'We can't risk wearing out the time paths, remember?' Frankie reminded Drew. 'We've got to send them together.'

'Oh yeah, that's right,' Drew replied sheepishly.

Then Frankie turned to his grandad. 'What will happen when we send them back?' asked Frankie anxiously.

'Hopefully they stay there,' replied Grandad.

'No, I mean ...' Frankie gulped, clutching the suitcase to his chest. 'When we brought Ping back here, we controlled her environment really carefully. But these two have roamed the streets, ridden trains, watched TV. Hell, Brynjar has even been *on* TV. Surely they've seen way too much?'

'Watch yer *language*, please –' Grandad growled.

'Frankie's right,' Drew whispered, as the magnitude of what they'd done suddenly hit him. **'This could totally disrupt history.'**

'And whose fault is that?' exploded Grandad. 'What possessed ye two doaty numpties to think that introducing a Viking to TV was a good idea?'

Frankie and Drew hung their heads. Frankie held his breath, waiting for Grandad to really lose it. But to his surprise, Grandad simmered down.

'Don't worry. I'm pretty sure I can fix it.'

Frankie eyed him suspiciously. 'How?'

But Grandad refused to explain. 'Let's just say there's been a wee upgrade made.'

'Ooh! Does the suitcase have Snapchat now?' Drew asked, a little too excitedly.

'Better than that, whatever that is,' Grandad said with a grin that made Frankie actually think things might turn out OK after all. But then, with Grandad, you could never be sure ...

# CHAPTER 19

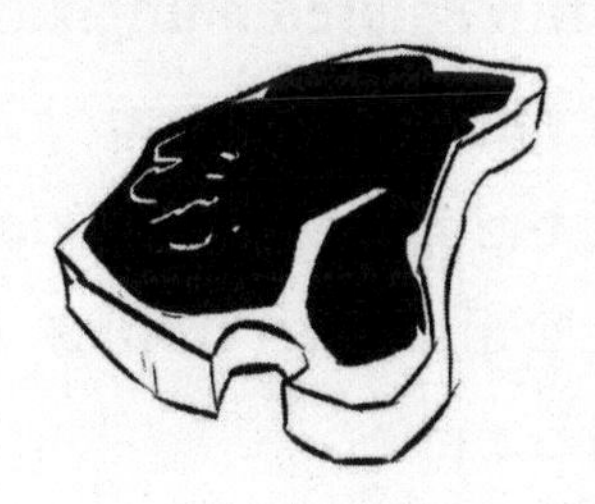

## THE GREAT ZOMBIE TRAP

There weren't many words spoken as Frankie, Grandad and Drew led Birger and Brynjar towards the school gates. Even the aroma of Principal Dawson's Korean barbecue booth didn't help soothe Frankie's nerves, although it did seem to excite both the Vikings (and Drew and Grandad too, truth be told).

Frankie was too nervous to feel hungry. What if Brynjar saw through their trap? What if he wasn't *really* scared of zombies? Or what if he

WAS scared of zombies but wasn't scared of kids in crappy costumes pretending to be zombies? Zombies with hula hoops, even?

For the first time ever, Frankie hoped that Lisa Chadwick and her cronies really nailed their zombie costumes.

Brynjar looked like he was starting to get a little impatient. He was muttering under his breath at Birger, who grimaced uncertainly.

'Not long now,' said Frankie, his stomach flip-flopping.

The loose plan was that Frankie would lead the Vikings *into* the parade so they would, hopefully, come face-to-face with Lisa Chadwick's zombie parade just as it was starting. Then, as soon as Brynjar freaked out and was distracted enough, Frankie could open the suitcase, set the co-ordinates and zap them back home.

As the group approached the entrance of the school, they saw people lined up on both sides of the outside basketball court, jockeying for the best position to view the parade.

Brynjar looked with concern at the milling crowd and growled something to Birger. Frankie hoped he wasn't about to go on another rampage. The parade was due to start in about ten minutes and Frankie did his best to calm him down. 'It's OK, they are just here for the feast.'

Birger understood enough to translate to Brynjar, who liked what he heard so much that he actually smiled. Frankie followed his nose and led his Nordic guests to the smoky Korean barbecue that Principal Dawson had been banging on about for weeks. On top of his Korean meats he also had hamburgers and sausages.

Looking up from his hotplate, Principal Dawson got a bit of a shock when he saw two large Viking teenagers standing in front of him.

'Oh, er ... hello there.'

Brynjar looked back at Principal Dawson, patted himself on the tummy with his huge hand, pointed at the giant steaks on the barbecue and uttered a single word. *'Slátr.'*

'Uh, he means *meat*,' guessed Frankie, quickly. 'These are my cousins from ... **very far away**. They don't speak English and they're really hungry.'

'Well, they've come to the right place! Would you like Korean spicy ribs or are you a banger-in-bread kind of Viking? Great costumes by the way, so authentic, although I see you've forgotten about the horned helmets,' Principal Dawson said enthusiastically. He lifted up a giant steak but, before he could put it on a plate, Brynjar grabbed it directly from the tongs with his bare hands and bit into it like he hadn't eaten for nine hundred years (technically, seeing as he'd skipped breakfast and lunch, he hadn't).

'You may need to set up a tab,' quipped Drew Bird, who had sneaked up to the front of the queue.

Grandad gave a shocked Principal Dawson

twenty dollars. 'Keep the meat coming.'

As the two Viking boys set about eating as much as ten regular men would, the school's public address system suddenly spluttered to life.

*'Ladies and gentlemen, welcome to the fifth annual St Monica's Halloween Parade, brought to you by Lisa Chadwick's Major Events, to raise money for anti-wrinkle cream for elephants ...'*

It was, of course, Lisa Chadwick herself speaking.

*'Before we kick things off tonight, just a reminder we will be holding a Spelling Bee next Wednesday to raise much-needed funds to train bees to make sugar-free honey ...'*

'Typical,' groaned Drew, rolling his eyes.

But Frankie had never been more relieved to hear Lisa's voice. 'Come on,' he muttered to Drew. 'We'd better get ready to join the parade. Make the most of the element of surprise with you-know-who.'

'Hang on a minute, you two,' said Principal

Dawson suddenly. 'You can't be in the parade. **You don't have costumes!**'

Frankie and Drew stared at each other in shock. They had been so focused on the returning the Vikings to their correct time that they had completely forgotten the number-one rule of the event: you had to have a costume to march in the parade.

'I've got your Viking helmet in my backpack – the one Birger gave you,' whispered Drew. 'How about I nip back home and get that old rug from Dad's shed?'

Frankie shook his head. 'There's no time! And the helmet isn't enough to make me look like a Viking. What are we going to do?'

Frankie turned back to Principal Dawson, who had just given the Viking boys another steak each and a sausage in bread to Grandad. 'Can't we just be in the parade anyway, without costumes?' he asked desperately.

But the principal shook his head. 'Absolutely

not! You know how Lisa feels about rules.'

Frankie was starting to feel panicky. He couldn't just push Birger and Brynjar towards a crowd of people waiting for the parade to start and hope they'd stay. Literally anything might happen. But where could he get a costume at such short notice?

There was a tap on his shoulder and Frankie turned to see his sister standing there, holding a big shopping bag.

'Did I hear you say you need costumes?' said Saint Lou.

Frankie looked eagerly at the bag. 'Yes! Do you have some?'

Maybe this was why his sister had been so secretive recently, he thought excitedly. Maybe she'd been busy making awesome costumes ... and now she was giving them to him and Drew!

Saint Lou saw his face and held up a hand. 'Don't get too excited,' she warned. 'All I've got here are some of your old ghost outfits. I thought there might be some kids down here who were **truly desperate** for something to wear.'

Drew and Frankie looked at each other, disappointed.

'Are we *that* desperate?' muttered Drew. As he spoke, Brynjar accidentally bit his finger while tearing into his steak, and let out a roar so loud that a nearby little kid dressed like Piglet squeaked in terror and dropped his pot of acorns.

'Yeah,' said Frankie quickly, putting the suitcase down for a moment so he could reach into the large plastic bag Lou was holding out. 'We ARE that desperate.'

The two boys pulled on the ghost costumes, both of which were so small that their legs clearly showed out the bottom. 'I had to cut some of the fabric off to use as cleaning rags,' Lou explained. Frankie ripped the eye holes of his costume wider so that he could see properly.

'You look great!' said Lou, but she had never been a good liar.

Frankie tried to swallow his disappointment. He had been so sure that he would win the competition this year. *But,* he reminded himself, *there are more important things at stake now.*

Drew nudged him. 'There's always next year.'

Frankie forced himself to smile (not that anyone could see it under his sheet). 'Yeah, exactly. Next year we'll come up with something amazing.'

Suddenly, a dramatic and ear-piercing scream came through the PA, which left the audience unsure if something terrible had happened or if this was simply part of the spooky theatrics (of course it was – this was Lisa Chadwick, Professional Drama Queen, don't forget).

Then Michael Jackson's 'Thriller' blasted

through the speakers and everyone relaxed. A huge grin spread across Birger's face and he began to shuffle from side to side, doing the same weird dance he'd done when he'd first met Frankie and Drew – one step forward, one step back, step to the side ...

'Not now, Birger,' hissed Frankie from under his costume. 'We don't have time.'

The ghostly Frankie ushered Birger and Brynjar towards the crowd of parade participants, with Drew bringing up the rear. Brynjar looked with interest at the strangely dressed people around him. At the moment, luckily, there were no zombies to be seen. Knowing Lisa Chadwick, she had kept them off to one side until the big moment – she really liked to make an entrance.

And then, as the music blared, a figure appeared from around the corner. Its face was very pale, except for some **dark shadows** around the eyes. Blood **dripped** from its mouth. Despite the zombified make-up, Frankie instantly recognised the figure as Lisa Chadwick because she was hula-hooping. Brynjar and Birger were looking in the opposite direction, and hadn't seen her yet.

He rolled his eyes. She really was the worst kind of show-off! Then an awful thought occurred to him: what if Brynjar *really* freaked out when he saw the zombies? He didn't know that they were just kids dressed up, after all. And what if his reaction was to go into attack mode?

Sure, Lisa and her cronies were annoying, but they didn't deserve to be put in that kind of danger. It suddenly struck Frankie that he might have made a **terrible mistake** bringing Brynjar here ...

# CHAPTER 20

# HALLO-SCREAM

The music got louder and the air was filled with the sound of evil laughter and blood-chilling moans. With an anxious knot rapidly growing in his stomach, Frankie waited for the madness to begin.

A moment later, zombies began pouring around the corner, all looking **completely terrifying** despite the fact they were dancing along to Michael Jackson's 'Thriller'. Their faces were deathly white, their hair was tangled and greasy, and they flashed their blood-covered teeth as they sung and danced towards the watching crowd. Frankie looked over to see how the Vikings were taking all of this.

Not well, it turned out. While Birger had gone white, Brynjar had stopped dead in his tracks, the smile disappearing off his face faster than a mother cleaning ice-cream off her baby's cheeks. He raised his huge hands to either side of his head and his mouth opened wide.

'NOOOOOO!' he yelled.

The crowd turned to stare, but then began laughing at the silly antics of the impressively dressed character, trying to guess who it was under that obviously fake beard.

But Brynjar wasn't laughing. Everywhere he looked there were *draugr*! It was his worst nightmare. Trembling, he didn't know whether to retreat or attack, and so he did what people often do when they feel like this (or at least, what Vikings do): he stood there, frozen in horror.

Grandad shuffled up to the boys (he recognised them by their shoes). 'That Viking is about to lose it,' he said urgently.

'I know,' said Frankie, nervously. 'Grandad – we need something for the Circle of Safety. Can you find something? And fast?'

'I could take my belt off,' offered Grandad, 'but then my pants would fall down, of course.'

'No, don't do that!' said Frankie quickly. The only thing that could possibly make the current situation worse would be having Grandad standing in the middle of the school's basketball court with his trousers around his knees.

'Would *that* do for the Circle of Safety?' asked Drew mischievously, pointing over at Lisa Chadwick's hula hoop.

Frankie snorted. 'That'd be *perfect!*' he said. 'Think you can get it?'

Through the (unevenly cut) holes in Drew's costume Frankie saw his friend's eyes twinkle. 'Leave it to me,' he said, and slunk away.

'I'll see if I can help,' said Grandad, shuffling away too, although Frankie was fairly sure he was heading back to the barbecue.

That left Frankie and the Vikings, one of whom was on the point of losing what little remained of his self-control.

As Frankie saw it, Brynjar was very close to doing one of two things:

1. Running away and hiding somewhere he'd never be found.
2. Charging at the dancing zombies with a blood-curdling shriek.

Neither option, Frankie knew, was good. Turning the key in the translator padlock and hoping with all his might that it would function properly, Frankie turned to Birger.

**'Birger,'** he said, seriously. 'It's nearly time to go home, but I need you to do something for me so I can make that happen. Can you please do it?'

Frankie could tell from the way Birger's wide eyes filled with tears that he understood the question. 'Here's what I need, Birger,' Frankie said, trying to work out how to explain it simply. 'In a moment I am going to hold up this box and open it. Coloured light will pour out. I need you to pretend that you are really scared of the zombies. *More* scared than Brynjar.'

Frankie started waving his arms about, to demonstrate.

Birger frowned. 'Why?' he said via the padlock (which, thank crikey, was working quite well at the moment).

'Because then, even though he is really scared of this box, your brother will come over to protect you,' Frankie said.

Birger shook his head. 'You are wrong,

*Frankiifisk*,' he said. 'My brother will *not* come over. He **hates** me.'

'No he doesn't,' said Frankie. He thought about how Lou had been there before, right when he needed her. 'That's the thing about siblings. You get mad at each other – sometimes *really* mad – but really, deep down, you ... you love each other.'

Birger looked like he wasn't at all sure he believed this, but eventually he nodded. 'I will try, *Frankiifisk*,' he said.

A shout came from nearby. **'Hey, Frankie!'** Frankie turned to see Drew pelting towards him from the other side of the basketball court, triumphantly holding a hula hoop aloft with a furious Lisa chasing behind.

'Give that back, Bird-brain!' she was yelling angrily. 'You're ruining everything!'

But Drew had no intention of doing that. Frankie calculated that it would take Drew a minute or so to weave through the crowd and get over to where he and Birger were standing. Hopefully by the time he arrived, Brynjar would be ready to get out of here too.

*Here goes* ... he thought, opening up the suitcase. He'd hoped that he could do this without too many people noticing. But if you open a suitcase and basically a rainbow pours out, it's pretty hard **not** to attract attention. It's even harder if the person dressed like a Viking standing next to you begins to act, very convincingly, as if he is terrified.

In no time at all, everyone in the whole of St Monica's was staring at Frankie and Birger – including Brynjar. But Brynjar was still frozen to the spot, and for one long, horrible moment, Frankie thought his plan had failed.

Then suddenly, Brynjar sprang to life.

'BIRGER!' he screamed and ran towards where Frankie was standing. Drew had managed to side-step the furious Lisa-Zombie and was now fast approaching from the opposite direction.

But would he be fast enough?

'Hurry!' Frankie screamed at Drew. He was more than a little worried that he was about to be flattened by an angry Viking.

As Brynjar charged up, he yelled something, which the padlock (after a burst of static) translated. 'I'll save you, Birger!'

Frankie squeezed his eyes shut, fully expecting to be attacked, but as the seconds passed and nothing happened, he gingerly opened one eye and then the other. He was greeted with

a very surprising sight.

Brynjar had flung his massive arms around his brother, who was more than a little stunned.

'Aw, how sweet!' a sweaty, red-faced Drew Bird managed to gasp as he too arrived, hula hoop clenched tightly in his hand.

But there was no time to appreciate the brotherly love. Frankie threw off his ghost costume, grabbed the hoop and pulled it down over himself, the suitcase and the two Vikings. The hoop worked like a lasso, trapping them all together. Frankie just managed to get his arms free and began typing the co-ordinates into the suitcase's keyboard.

'Hold on! Ye'll need these,' Grandad called, hurrying up to the group holding a half-eaten sausage in one hand and a pair of sunglasses in the other. Frankie recognised them as the same octagon-shaped pair Grandad had been wearing in the Forbidden Shed the other day.

'Use these, Frankie!' Grandad said, tossing the glasses to him. 'We just finished making them! Put 'em on and press the yellow button in the corner just before you go.'

There was no time for questions. Frankie jammed the glasses on his face and kept typing like mad.

Just then, there was a burst of colour in the sky as Mr Hedge's annual Halloween fireworks display got underway. Eyes were directed skyward, which gave Frankie just the window of opportunity he needed.

'Happy travels!' he called to Grandad and Drew and slammed his hand down on the yellow button.

The crowd 'oohed' and 'aahed' at the fireworks (which were good, but nowhere near as good as the northern lights) and didn't even notice that Frankie Fish and the two Vikings simply **vanished** as the hula hoop dropped and spun on the ground. At least, *most* people didn't.

'See you soon, Frankie Fish,' whispered Drew Bird. 'I hope.'

# CHAPTER 21

## BRYNJAR AND THE BEAR

Frankie was pretty used to time travel now. He had travelled more with the Sonic Suitcase than he had on an aeroplane.

But this trip was a little different.

There was, as usual, all kinds of weirdness whizzing around them (backwards, of course). But this time there was also an array of colours spinning around them like they were trapped in a rainbow cyclone – or like they were in the middle of the aurora borealis.

The full intensity of the colours was dulled a bit for Frankie, who was wearing the sunglasses Grandad had given him, but Birger and Brynjar got the full blast. They were mesmerised by them, staring in wide-eyed amazement as they swirled around. Until, suddenly –

**THUD!!**

Trees that smelt like Christmas, animal dung and distant smoke.

That was what Frankie could smell as he scrambled to his feet, a little woozy but relieved he hadn't landed face-down in **reindeer poop**. He wiped some mud (he hoped it was mud, anyway) from his T-shirt as he looked around, trying to work out where they were, exactly.

It was night time, in the forest near the gnarled tree. Overhead, the aurora was rippling across the sky, just as it had been when they left.

Frankie grinned to himself. Despite the stress of the hasty departure, it looked like he had typed in the return co-ordinates perfectly. They had returned to the Viking era only minutes after they had departed. **Bulls-eye!**

Nearby lay their Circle of Safety from the trip before, which had one large white stone dislodged. Birger was in it, as he had been when they left, but now he was sitting up rather than sprawled out unconscious. And Brynjar was right beside them, axe gripped tightly in his hand. Both of the Viking teenagers seemed momentarily frozen in place and were both staring, confused, at Frankie.

Frankie turned the key in the padlock just in time for it to translate Birger's words. 'Where did *Dru-Børd* go? He was right here!' and then, 'Get off me, Brynjar!' as he pushed his brother away.

Frankie felt the knot in his stomach unravel a bit. The Vikings' memories of their time-travelling trip had been entirely wiped. That must be what the glasses are for, he realised. *If you wear them, they protect your memory. And anyone who doesn't wear them has no idea they've just travelled through time.* He felt a **pang** of appreciation for his grandad's recent inventing streak.

The relief that flooded through Frankie, however, quickly vanished when Brynjar turned to Birger and picked up yesterday's shouting argument as if they'd been having it moments before (because as far as they knew, they had). 'You should have protected our father! He is dead because of you.'

Frankie felt that familiar **heaviness** weighing on his heart. The boys' father was still dead, it was still his and Drew's fault and the brothers were still fighting.

Brynjar's expression was bordering on dangerous when the sound of twigs snapping and the rustling of leaves caused all three boys to look around sharply. Frankie's heart thumped against his chest. Was another bear coming? Brynjar lifted his axe and Birger leapt to his feet.

The branches of the gnarled tree were pushed to one side and a figure walked through. Not a bear, but a Viking woman. Frankie recognised her as the particularly strong-looking one who had been handing out meat at the funeral feast. She strode over and stood between the brothers, her arms outstretched, her expression extremely serious. As she began to speak, Frankie held the padlock up to his ear, desperate to understand as much as possible.

'Brynjar!' the woman admonished the larger boy. 'You are not being honest. Tell your brother the true story of what happened with the bear.'

'I don't know what you're talking about, Sigrún,' growled Brynjar, but Frankie saw that he looked worried.

The Viking woman – Sigrún – folded her arms. 'Well then, I will tell him,' Sigrún turned to Birger. 'I was in the woods earlier, collecting wood,' she explained. 'And I saw a bear – the one that killed your father. It was followed by two bear cubs. The three of them were foraging for berries quite calmly, but when I saw those cubs I knew I had to leave – and quickly. There is **nothing** in the forest as dangerous as a mother bear. She will do anything to protect her young if she thinks they are being threatened.'

'How do you know it was the same bear that killed our father?' snapped Brynjar. Frankie noticed he was acting very strangely, shifting uneasily from foot to foot.

'Because when it stretched up to reach some fruit I saw the mark of the aurora on its belly,' Sigrún replied.

'Go on,' said Birger. He was standing very still, listening intently.

'As I was about to leave,' Sigrún continued, 'someone came through the trees into the clearing where the bear family was foraging.'

She pointed her finger at Brynjar. 'You. When you saw the bears you shouted in fright and startled them. And of course the mother bear did what mother bears do: she reared up onto her hind legs to protect her cubs.'

Birger turned to face his brother. 'Brynjar? Is this true?'

Brynjar said nothing. His face was like stone.

'He screamed again as the bear came towards him, enraging the bear even more,' Sigrún went on, her eyes fixed on Birger. 'And just as it was almost upon him, your father burst through the trees. At the very last moment he pushed Brynjar out of the way, into some nearby bushes. Your father fought valiantly against the bear, but he was no match for the furious mother.' Sigrún put one of her huge, strong-looking hands on Birger's shoulder. 'He didn't die in vain, Birger. Your father died a **hero**, saving your brother.'

Frankie's gob was well and truly smacked. He couldn't believe that Brynjar had been there the whole time! And he had let Birger believe it had been *his* fault.

*If Lou did something like that, I'd never forgive her!* thought Frankie hotly, although he knew that the situation was extremely unlikely to arise.

Birger turned to his brother, his eyes wide. Frankie expected him to go crazy and yell angrily at Brynjar. But Birger stayed calm, as he always did. 'Brynjar ... is this true?'

For a moment Brynjar did not react at all. And then, quite suddenly, he dropped to his knees, covering his face with his hands and sobbing heart-wrenchingly. 'Yes, it's true. I – I was too **ashamed** to tell you. I was a **coward**. I caused our father's death. And I was afraid to tell you. I th-thought you would never forgive me.'

Frankie's mouth dropped open as Birger went and knelt beside his brother. 'Of course I forgive you,' he said, softly. 'It was a terrible accident. A mistake. It could have just as easily happened to me, or Sigrún, or anyone. It's not your fault. I don't blame you and I know our father doesn't either.'

Brynjar turned up his tear-stained face to his brother. 'How do you know that?'

Birger pointed skywards. 'Because look at how brightly the aurora is shining, how intense the colours are! It's a sign from our father, watching from Valhalla, that he loves us now and forever.'

Brynjar looked doubtful for a moment, then slowly nodded.

Birger helped him to his feet and the two Viking brothers embraced. Finally Birger held his brother at arm's length and said, 'So, from now on we'll be honest with each other? And you are not only protecting me. I am protecting you.'

At that moment the padlock gave a little static-y wheeze and stopped working. But it didn't matter. Frankie could tell from Brynjar's expression what his answer was.

The brothers and the woman headed back to the village, leaving a slightly teary-eyed Frankie sitting in the Circle of Safety. Quickly, he made sure the stones were all in place before whispering those now-famous words: 'Happy travels.'

# CHAPTER 22

## A FINAL MYSTERY REVEALED

Frankie returned to St Monica's Primary to find Lisa Chadwick's fifth annual Halloween Parade coming to its usual conclusion, with Principal Dawson about to present the Best Costume award. He was standing in front of the microphone with the rest of the judging panel behind them.

Frankie frowned. *Hang on* ... There was something different about the judges. Where was Lisa's mum, for one thing? And why was

Connie from the Cocoa Pit standing there? The answer to that question came a moment later, from Principal Dawson himself.

'Before I announce this year's winner, I'd like to thank Connie Cole for stepping in as a last-minute emergency judge for us,' he said. 'We hope that Mrs Chadwick recovers very soon. Who would have thought that milk from a lactose-intolerant cow could cause such an extreme digestive complaint?'

Connie waved as the crowd clapped, and when she caught Frankie's eye she gave him a huge grin.

Principal Dawson cleared his throat. 'The winner of the Best Costume award and the recipient of the one-hundred-dollar voucher at the Cocoa Pit this year goes to ... drum roll please!'

A sense of *déjà vu* came over Frankie. He was pretty sure he could guess the name about to be read out – someone whose name started with an

'L' and ended with an 'isa Chadwick' – and he steeled himself for the disappointment.

'Frankie Fish!' said Principal Dawson.

'What?' Frankie whispered. That was not the name he'd been expecting.

**'WHAT?!'**

screamed Lisa Chadwick-Thatcher.

That was clearly not the name Lisa Chadwick had been expecting, either. '*I* should have won!' he could hear her screeching. 'That Bird-brain stole my hula hoop! I demand a re-count!'

But no-one was listening. They were all too busy congratulating Frankie and cheering in delight. (It turned out Frankie wasn't the only person sick of Lisa winning every year.)

Drew pushed his way through the crowd until he was by Frankie's side and began thumping Frankie vigorously on the back. 'Stop standing there like a stunned mullet and go get our prize, Frankie!' he yelled.

Feeling like he was in a trance, Frankie stumbled towards the stage, a grin spreading over his face. 'There must be some mistake,' he stammered as he finally made it to where the judges were lined up, waiting. 'Ghosts don't win Best Costume competitions.'

'Ah, but ghost *magicians* do!' said Connie Coal, her eyes twinkling. 'Most people were distracted by the fireworks, but *I* saw that amazing disappearing trick you pulled off. One minute you and those two Viking boys were there and then next you'd gone. I have **no idea** how you did it! You absolutely deserve to win.'

Frankie felt his face going red. 'It was nothing, really,' he said quickly, and grabbed the Cocoa Pit voucher from Principal Dawson's hand.

**'SPEECH! SPEECH! SPEECH!'** chanted the crowd.

Principal Dawson pressed the microphone into Frankie's hand. Looking out at that sea of faces, Frankie's mouth felt completely dry and his tongue seemed to have twisted itself into a pretzel. Then he spotted two faces in the crowd that made his nerves disappear.

'I'd like to thank my sister Lou, and my best mate Drew Bird, for all his assistance with the, um ... *magic trick*. You have no idea how far we went to win this. **Drew, milkshakes are on me!'**

$10

Then Frankie dropped the mic and strode off the stage to the cheers of the entire school.

(Well, the entire school minus one, that is. Can you guess who?)

It was a week later and Frankie and Drew had barely spoken to Grandad. As they'd come really close to **seriously disrupting** the history of the world, Frankie thought it was best that they give Grandad some space. He and Drew hadn't even had their first pig-out meal at the Cocoa Pit yet.

But that all changed the following Sunday morning when the Fish family phone rang.

'It's your grandad for you, Frankie!' called Frankie's mum.

Frankie frowned. Grandad was calling him? That was strange. Usually it was Nanna Fish who made the phone calls. He felt a twinge in his tummy. He really hoped Grandad wasn't calling him from Ancient Greece or the Jurassic period asking for help.

'Hello?' Frankie said hesitantly.

'Hey kiddo, how are ye feeling?' Grandad

sounded chipper. Suspiciously so.

'I'm good, I guess,' replied Frankie cautiously.

'That's great,' shouted Grandad.

'Um, Grandad, did you double-dose your medication or something?' Frankie blurted.

'Don't be a fool. I'm just happy to talk to my grandson!'

'So you don't need me to come rescue you from anywhere?'

'Ye and yer jokes,' Grandad chuckled. 'No, nothing like that ...'

Frankie breathed a sigh of relief. Maybe he was worrying for nothing.

'But I would like to meet with ye today,' added Grandad. 'There's something I need to, er, come clean about. A **big secret** that it's high time ye knew about.'

Frankie's first instinct was to pretend the phone line had been disconnected. Grandad was acting so strangely. He really wasn't sure he wanted to know what Grandad's big secret was.

But he also knew it was probably better that he found out sooner rather than later.

'Sure,' he said. 'I'll come over now.'

'Oh and bring yer friend, what's-his-name, along if ye like.'

'Drew Bird?'

'Yes, bring ol' Bird-brain along.'

'Well, in that case, how about we meet at the Cocoa Pit? Our treat.'

'Good idea!' Grandad said abruptly, and then hung up, leaving his grandson very curious and more than a little nervous about what was going to be revealed.

The doorbell dinged as Frankie walked into the Cocoa Pit, where he found Grandad and Nanna Fish sitting together in a booth.

Frankie was relieved that Nanna was there, as surely it meant that Grandad's big secret wasn't that he had a girlfriend (not that Frankie had ever truly believed that anyway, but Drew had planted the idea in his mind and sometimes it was hard to ignore Drew's ideas).

Speaking of Drew, he was sitting alongside Nanna Fish, already halfway through a giant cookie. 'Frankie, sweetheart!' cooed Nanna, making an even bigger fuss than usual over seeing him.

Frankie's nervous feeling doubled in size. Something wasn't right.

'Grandad, what's going on? This is weirding me out.'

'OK, lads,' said Grandad, leaning back. 'I won't waste anymore of ye time, as we all know just how precious time is.'

'You're going to tell us to stop time-travelling, aren't you?' Frankie interrupted. 'You're going to **ban us** from using the **Sonic Suitcase**. And to be honest, Grandad, I think you're right. We put lives in danger with this latest fiasco –

Birger's life, Brynjar's, our own and even Lisa Chadwick's. So let me say that I agree with you. We should **destroy** the Sonic Suitcase.'

There was a long, quiet pause while everyone looked from Frankie, to Grandad, and then back to Frankie.

'What a load of crapola,' Grandad roared.

'What?' said Frankie.

'What?' repeated Drew.

'Crapola,' repeated Grandad loudly. 'It's Italian for *crap*.'

'I don't think that's true –' said Frankie.

'Why would I stop ye using the suitcase?' Grandad barrelled on. 'We have one of the greatest inventions of all time in our possession. Could ye imagine if Alexander Graham Bell told everybody not to use the telephone or if Edison said don't use lightbulbs? No, that's a silly way to think ...'

'Then why are we here, exactly?' asked Drew, who was now out of cookies.

'I admit we do definitely need to make things safer. We need somebody we trust to keep an eye on us, keep us **safe**, keep *everybody* safe. Someone who can help update the Sonic Suitcase. Someone with a strong sense of responsibility and teamwork. Now, who is the person best suited to fill that role?'

Frankie scratched his head and uttered the only name he could think of. 'Nanna Fish?'

Nanna snorted and shook her head. 'No thank you, dearie,' she said. 'The Sonic ooza-majig is *not* for me.'

'No, Nanna's time-travelling days finished after that trip to Imperial China,' Grandad said. 'I've been working with someone for a little while now, and they've already shown themselves to be perfect for the job. The Memory Wipe Sunglasses, the translating padlock and the coloured light display were all her work. I think she's going to be a great addition to the team. And so from now on, she must be involved in any adventures you plan ...'

Frankie and Drew looked at each other, eyebrows raised. **She?**

Just then, the cafe's doorbell tinkled brightly again. Grandad looked up and his eyes sparkled. 'Why don't ye say hello to our new Head of Time-Travel Logistics?'

Curiously, Frankie turned. Walking towards their booth, carrying the Sonic Suitcase, was none other than ...

His sister, Saint Lou.

'Hey brother,' Lou said with an excited but slightly nervous smile. 'So, where to next?'

Frankie's jaw dropped. 'Oh, crapola.'

**THE END**

# ABOUT THE AUTHOR

Peter Helliar is the best-selling author of the *Frankie Fish* series and one of Australia's favourite comedians. He lives in Melbourne with his wife and three kids.

The Gold Logie nominee co-hosts the award-winning news and current affairs program *The Project*, and wrote and starred in the new TV comedy *How To Stay Married*, both on Network Ten. His latest family comedy show is *The Complete History of Better Books*. He plans to interview Frankie Fish on *The Project* one day, in what will hopefully be an exclusive.

# THANKS!

Many thanks to Brij, Liam, Aidan and Oscar. My team at Token Artists: Kevin, Dioni, Helen, Sam, Kathleen. The amazing people at Hardie Grant Egmont, led by Marisa Pintado: Luna Soo, Meredith Badger, Penelope White, Pooja Desai, Kristy Lund-White, Haylee Collins, Julia Kumschick and the entire sales team. Lesley Vamos, whose drawings bring Frankie and co. to life! Most importantly of all, thanks to all the kids who have taken Frankie, Drew, Grandad, Nanna and Saint Lou into their homes, hearts and heads. I continually think of you when I am writing these books. Your passion and eagerness to read has kept Frankie and the gang going.

Finally, thank you to the librarians across the country – and indeed the world – who encourage reading and who keep putting books into the hands of kids.

Pete

BOOK ONE

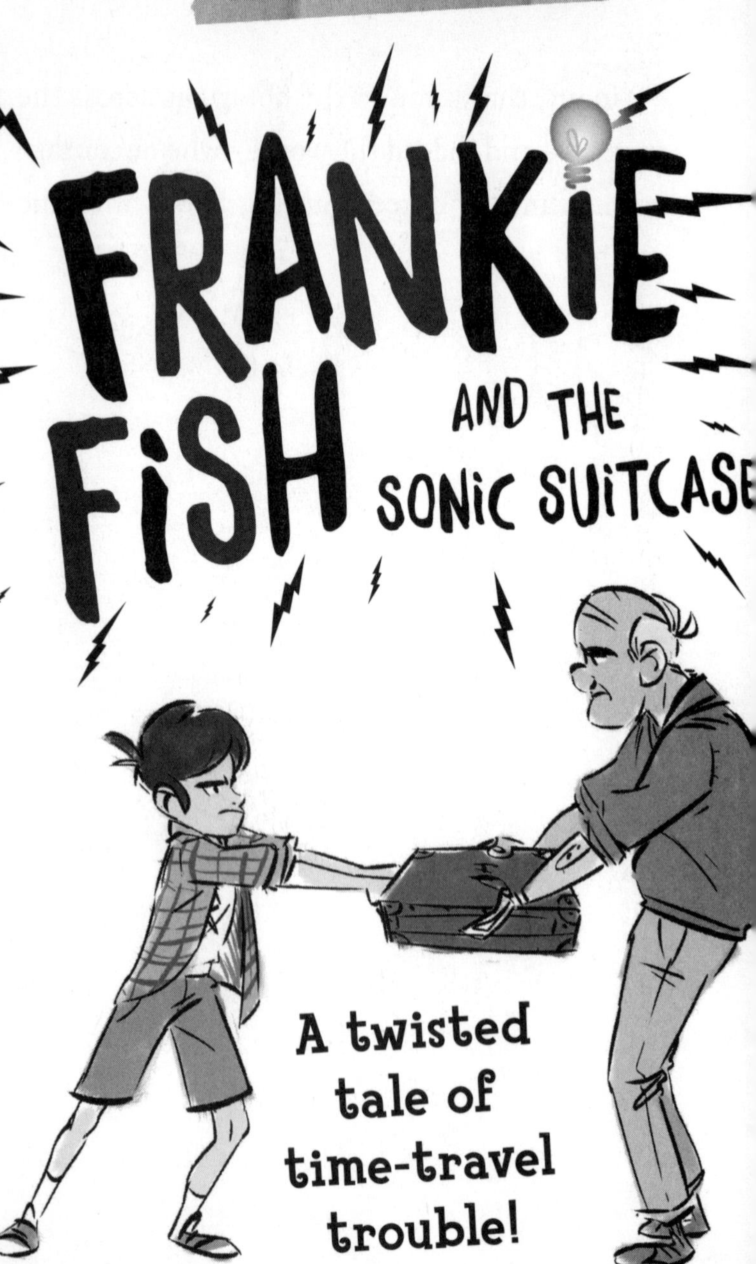
FRANKIE FISH
AND THE SONIC SUITCASE
A twisted tale of time-travel trouble!

What do you do when your cranky-pants grandad builds a time machine and accidentally deletes the whole family? If you're Frankie Fish, you race against the clock to save them!

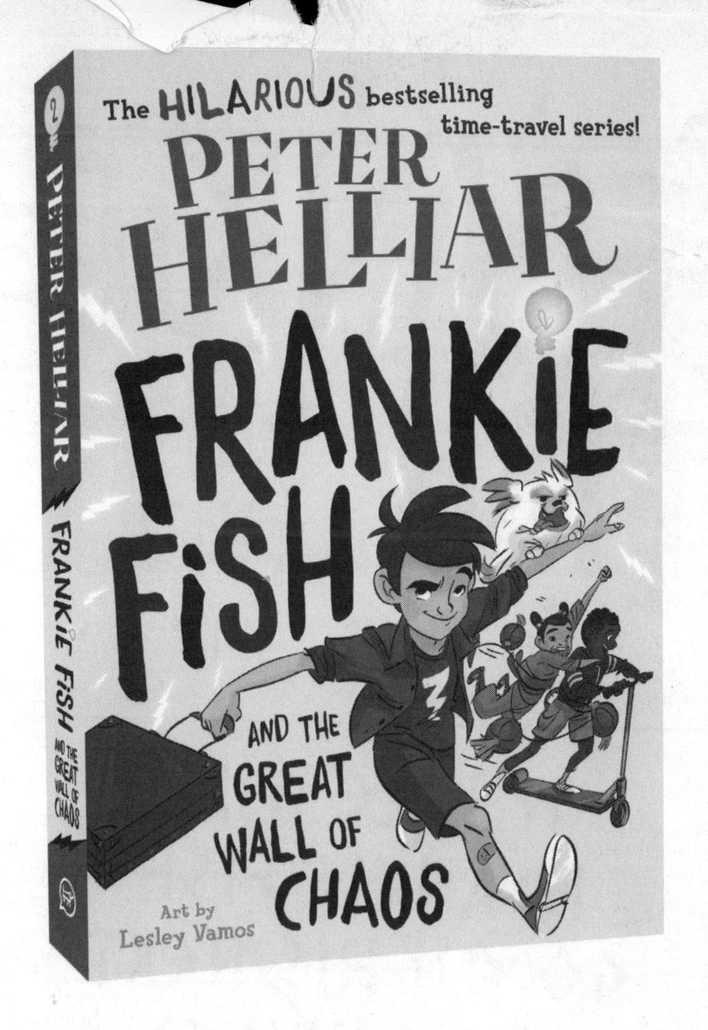


Frankie and Drew have got hold of Grandad's time machine, but it's no laughing matter. Grandad and Nanna have disappeared to seventeenth-century China, and it's up to these two pranksters to save them!

# FRANKIE FISH

## BOOK FOUR

WHERE WILL FRANKIE FISH GO ON HIS NEXT ADVENTURE?

COMING IN 2019!